NIGHTMARE ON MAIN STREET

Just as Clint burst into the parlor, he saw the gunslinger grab his beautiful hostage by the hair, pull her off the floor, and drag her to the window. He had to act fast.

He barked the bandit's name.

The gunman whirled, starting to bring his gun to bear on Clint Adams. He was partially shielded by his hostage, but Clint knew he'd never get another chance. He fired, and the bullet drilled the killer in the forehead. His eyes went blank, and his hands opened. His gun fell to the floor. But the rest of his crew had brought their guns around—aimed directly at Clint's chest . . .

DON'T MISS THESE
ALL-ACTION WESTERN SERIES
FROM THE BERKLEY PUBLISHING GROUP

THE GUNSMITH by J. R. Roberts
Clint Adams was a legend among lawmen, outlaws, and ladies. They called him . . . the Gunsmith.

LONGARM by Tabor Evans
The popular long-running series about U.S. Deputy Marshal Long—his life, his loves, his fight for justice.

LONE STAR by Wesley Ellis
The blazing adventures of Jessica Starbuck and the martial arts master, Ki. Over eight million copies in print.

SLOCUM by Jake Logan
Today's longest-running action western. John Slocum rides a deadly trail of hot blood and cold steel.

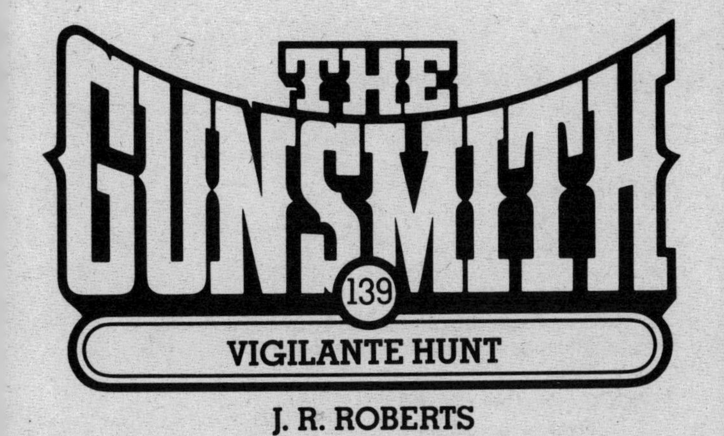

J. R. ROBERTS

JOVE BOOKS, NEW YORK

VIGILANTE HUNT

A Jove Book / published by arrangement with
the author

PRINTING HISTORY
Jove edition / July 1993

ISBN: 0-515-11138-4

Jove Books are published by The Berkley Publishing Group,
200 Madison Avenue, New York, New York 10016.
The name "JOVE" and the "J" logo
are trademarks belonging to Jove Publications, Inc.

PRINTED IN THE UNITED STATES OF AMERICA

10 9 8 7 6 5 4 3 2 1

ONE

The six men who robbed the Bank of Broken Back, Kansas, were smart about it. They rode into town separately, or in twos. The first two rode in at eight A.M. and by two P.M. they were all there.

The leader of the bank robbers was named Sam Cade. He rode into town at noon, and took up residence at the Broken Back Saloon to await the arrival of the last two of his gang. He bought a beer and nursed it, doing nothing to bring attention to himself. Later, no one would remember the stranger who spent so much time over a single beer.

Across the street two of his men sat on a bench in front of the general store. There was one man leaning against a hitching post by the hardware store. The fifth man actually sat on a chair in front of the bank.

All five of them had left their horses near the bank, but not clustered together outside. The animals would have attracted attention all hitched up together that way. This way they were innocently tied, and yet within easy reach of the bank.

Cade was waiting now for the sixth man, the key man in this robbery. He was the one who had given them the information about the Bank of Broken Back. He was the one who had told them *when* the bank should be hit, *when* there would be enough money in the small bank to make the robbery worthwhile.

From his table Cade could see out the front window of the saloon. As he sat and watched, the sixth man came riding in, ambling really, not hurrying at all. Cade knew the man was nervous, but he had been carefully instructed not to betray his nervousness so he wouldn't attract attention.

Sam Cade was the only one who knew the names of the entire gang. There were a couple of men he had used before, and they knew each other, but that was because they were brothers. They didn't know any of the others, though, the way Cade did. They were all handpicked by Cade, and all but one had been on jobs with him before.

The new man was the sixth man, the one who was actually *from* Broken Back. Cade usually put his gang together, and then picked someone from the town, someone with inside information.

That was the sixth man, the one who had just ridden in. Now that he was here, the robbery could commence.

• • •

Cade came out of the saloon and cast a slow glance the street at the Dalman brothers. Avery Dalman nodded, and nudged his brother Carl with his elbow.

Cade started walking down the street towards the bank, and the Dalman brothers did the same across the street.

The sixth man was still riding towards the bank, and he rode right up to it and dismounted. He would be the first man into the bank because no one would be suspicious of him. After all, he was *from* Broken Back, wasn't he?

From the other direction came the other two men, Jimmy Payne and Joe Daniels. They were waking slowly, so as not to attract too much attention.

Once the sixth man entered the bank, Cade would be the next one in, followed by the Dalman brothers. Jimmy Payne would follow them. Joe Daniels would stand watch outside, so they wouldn't be surprised by anyone.

The five men had all been through this exercise before, although never as the same group. Cade alternated his people, never using the same ones on two jobs in a row. The Dalman brothers had worked with him more than any of the others.

As Cade entered the bank the sixth man was engaging one of the two tellers in conversation. Cade waked up to the second teller's cage.

The Dalman boys entered and moved to either side of the door.

Jimmy Payne entered and walked over to where the bank manager was sitting. He was the first one to draw his gun and speak.

He took it out of his holster, pointed it at the man who was identified by a name plate on his desk as Walter Devine, Bank Manager, and said, "No sudden moves, Mr. Devine, or you'll be meeting your maker much sooner than you thought."

"Wha-what is this?" Devine stammered.

Payne smiled and said, "What does it look like? This is a holdup."

When the sheriff of Broken Back heard the shot he was seated at his desk in his office, eating a meal he had brought over from the Blue Belle Cafe. He was only halfway through it, and in fact the sound of the shot jarred a large piece of stew from his fork and sent it tumbling to the floor.

"Shit!" he swore, standing up.

He hated wasting food.

He grabbed his hat and ran for the door. Whoever had made him drop that piece of meat was going to pay.

By the time he was through the door the other shots had started.

TWO

When Sam Cade walked through the front doors of the Bank of Broken Back, Clint Adams was in bed with Sherry Lance. Clint had been in Broken Back for about a week, and most of his time in bed had been spent with the dark-haired beauty he had met on the second day in town.

All during the first evening in town the girls at the Broken Back Saloon had been trying to get Clint Adams's attention, but the truth was he had noticed Sherry when he first rode into town. She had been standing outside a shop that turned out to be hers, a store from which she sold hats and dresses to the women of the town. She had been outside fanning herself with a white fan, and their eyes had met and held as he rode by in his gunsmithing rig.

So enamored of the dark-haired woman had Clint been that, even though they hadn't met and he didn't know her name, he was thinking about her that first evening in the saloon.

The next day he made it a point to meet her, going so far as to enter her store and pose as a customer. The pose amused her.

"Surely you can't be here to buy something," she'd said to him with a small, amused smile on her face.

"And why not?"

"Well . . . do you have a wife to buy something for?" she'd asked.

"No."

"A girlfriend, then?"

"No," he'd said. He knew many women, and *many* of them were his friends, but none of them were *girl*friends in the way that she was referring to.

"Well then . . ."

"Suppose I told you I wanted to buy something for you," he'd said.

"That's silly," she'd replied.

"Why?"

"Because you don't *know* me."

"All right, then," he'd said, "let's *get* to know each other, and *then* maybe I'll buy you something."

So they had gotten to know each other, and continued to get to know each other over the next five days, and he still hadn't bought her anything.

They had just finished making love when Sherry mentioned that to him.

"You've been in town now for what, seven days?"

"We met on the second."

"So we've known each other for six," she said, "and you *still* haven't bought me anything."

She was sitting up in bed next to him, the sheet gathered around her waist. Her skin was very pale, and her breasts were very full, tipped with brown nipples. *So* pale was her skin that he could see the fine lines of her veins underneath the surface.

"I'm still trying to decide," he said, "what you deserve."

"Oh, really?" she asked.

"Yes," he said. "It's got to be something oh, something *big*, something . . . um, something that no one else has."

She slid her hand beneath the sheet until she was holding his penis. As she held it, and massaged it, it began to swell.

"What did you have in mind?" she asked, teasingly wetting her lips.

"Well, *that*, of course," he said, "but I was talking about something that I'd have to *buy* for you."

"Something from my store?" she asked, removing her hand from beneath the sheet.

"Of course," he said. "Where else would I buy it?"

"Well, then," she said, "just buy the most

expensive item in the store."

"And what would that be?"

She thought a moment and then said, "How about a dress that I got from New York, but it *came* all the way from Paris, France."

"A dress? Is it pretty?"

"It's beautiful."

"What color is it?"

"Yellow."

He shook his head. "No."

"Why not?"

"Yellow is not your color."

"Oh? What is my color?"

He thought a moment and then said, "Lavender."

"Lavender?"

"Yes," he said, "it's like purple, only more—"

"I *know* what color lavender is," she said, cutting him off. "You are the most *surprise*-filled man I have ever known."

"Why is that?"

"Because lavender *is* my color," she said, "and I don't know another man who would ever *know* that."

He was trying to figure out how to take a bow while lying in bed when they heard the first shot.

"What was that?" she asked, looking around in surprise.

"A shot."

She looked at him and said, "A shot?"

"That's what it sounded like to me."

He knew a shot when he heard one. He also

knew that reacting to a shot had often gotten him into a lot of trouble. This time he was determined to stay where he was. The town had law. Let *them* react to the shot.

That was when they heard the other shots, a virtual barrage. Sherry Lance leaped off the bed and ran to the window.

"Oh, my God," she said. "Somebody's robbing the bank."

He frowned, still determined to let the law handle the situation.

She turned to him and asked, "Aren't you gonna do anything?"

"This town has a sheriff," he said. "He'll do something."

"Unless it has something to do with food," she said, "the sheriff is incompetent."

He shrugged and said, "Someone voted him into office."

She put her fists on her hips, a move that caused her breasts to jiggle.

"Clint Adams," she said, "*I* have money in that bank!"

Clint frowned, resisted a moment longer, but finally wilted beneath her steely gaze.

"Oh," he said, throwing back the sheet, "all right . . ."

So much for minding his own business.

THREE

By the time Clint got down to the street the gun battle was in full swing. He ran towards the bank and saw a fat man down on one knee, his hat on the ground, exchanging shots with five men in front of the bank. If this was the local sheriff, then Sherry Lance had been wrong about him. He *was* fat, but he wasn't incompetent. Of course, he wasn't *hitting* anyone either.

Clint, hatless and shirtless—although he *had* taken the time to pull on his pants and boots—joined the fray even before he reached the lawman. He fired once, and one of the robbers spun, grabbing his shoulder. One of the other men grabbed hold of him and supported him.

"Wha—Who the hell—" the sheriff said, as Clint came up next to him.

"Keep shooting, Sheriff," Clint said. "There's still only two of us."

The robbers, seeing another gun join the battle, decided to pull out. After all, they had their money already. All they had to do was get away with it.

"Pull out," Sam Cade shouted.

"But Sam," Jimmy Payne said, "there's only two of 'em."

"Let's go," Avery Dalman said. "My brother's hit."

Sam Cade eyed Jimmy Payne angrily and said, "We're pullin' out." The man would pay later for calling him by name.

Cade moved alongside the Dalmans and helped Avery get his brother up onto a horse.

"They're pullin' out!" the sheriff shouted. He sounded surprised.

Clint fired his last shot. It missed because the outlaw's horse suddenly darted to the left. He had to reload now, as did the sheriff, and the gang took advantage and mounted up. One of them unsheathed his rifle and held Clint and the sheriff pinned down while the others rode off. He then followed.

"There was too many," Clint said to the sheriff.

"We can chase them," the sheriff said.

Clint looked around and didn't see any horses. Whatever animals *had* been there had pulled loose when the shooting started and had run off.

"On what?" he asked, and the sheriff looked around helplessly.

"Don't you have any deputies?" Clint asked.

The sheriff, getting up for the first time, towered over Clint. He was not just a fat man. He was *huge,* standing at least six-six and weighing four hundred pounds at least.

"I do," the sheriff said, and the anger in his eyes was so naked that Clint was glad that *he* was not one of the man's deputies right at that moment.

"Well," Clint said, holstering his gun, "I guess you better find them."

"Hey," the sheriff said, but Clint turned and started to walk away. He saw coming towards him a fully dressed—and *angry*—Sherry Lance.

"They got away," she said, her tone accusing.

"There were too many of them," he said helplessly, "and the sheriff's deputies weren't around."

"Aren't you gonna chase them?" she asked.

"That's up to the sheriff," Clint said. "He'll have to get a posse together."

"You'll go with him, of course," she said.

"No, Sherry," Clint said, "I won't."

"But . . . but they might have my money."

"If they do," he said, "it'll be up to the sheriff to get it back. It's not my business."

"You—" she said, glaring at him. At a loss for words, she pushed past him and rushed to the bank to see if the robbers *had* gotten away with her money.

Clint had the feeling that he and Sherry Lance had gotten to know each other as well as they were going to.

FOUR

Clint walked from the scene of the bank robbery to the livery stable. He had just made a spur-of-the-moment decision to leave Broken Back the next morning. He wanted to be gone before the town exploded.

As he entered the livery, the first thing he saw was the liveryman wrestling with a mule.

"Need some help?" Clint asked.

"Fool mule," the man said.

Clint helped the man calm the mule and get him into a stall.

"Thanks," the man said. "When he gets like that he's hard to handle."

"What's his problem?" Clint asked.

"Oh, he was out back when the shooting started and like to went wild," the man said. Clint noticed that the man would not meet his eyes.

"Well, he seems calm enough now," Clint said.

"Listen, I'd like my rig, team, and horse ready in the morning. I'll be leaving."

The man rubbed his hand over his grizzled jaw and answered without looking at Clint.

"Well, your team and your horse, now that's no problem."

Clint frowned and asked, "And what's wrong with my rig? It was fine when I got here."

"Well . . ."

"Where is it?"

"Out back," the man said, "where you left it."

"Let me see it," Clint said, starting for the back door.

"Now, mister, take it easy," the liveryman said, running after him. "It were an accident . . ."

Clint went out the back door and looked at his rig. For a moment it seemed fine, but then he saw that it was listing to one side.

"What the hell . . ." he said, and walked over for a closer look.

As he came around he saw that one of the wheels was in pieces, which was why the rig was leaning to that side.

"What the hell happened here?" he demanded, looking at the liveryman.

"Like I said," the man replied, "my mule was out here when the shooting started and he like to went wild."

"Are you telling me that your mule kicked my wheel to pieces?"

"Uh, yeah, that's what I'm tellin' you. I'm really sorry, mister—"

"Never mind your apologies," Clint said. "Do you have another wheel?"

The man looked at Clint, then looked away and said quickly, "No."

"Can you get one?"

The man brightened and said, "Sure . . . but I got to order it."

"How long will that take?"

Now the man looked away again and said, "Oh, prolly about two weeks."

"Two weeks?"

"Or mebbe three . . ."

"Jesus!" Clint said, staring at his crippled rig. "Why couldn't you put your mule someplace else?"

"Mister, I *said* I was sorry . . ."

"Never mind," Clint said, "never mind . . . just order the damn wheel."

"Okay . . ."

Clint started to walk away and the man called out, "Hey, mister, don't you want to know what your new wheel is gonna cost?"

Clint hunched his shoulders, whirled around, and bellowed, "What?"

FIVE

At the bank the sheriff was trying to deal with the bank manager, the employees, some of the customers, and with Sherry Lance, who was still very concerned about her money.

"I'm afraid, Miss Lance," the bank manager said, "that *all* of the depositors' money was taken, not only yours."

"Well," Sherry Lance said, "I'm worried about *my* money."

At that moment the sheriff's two deputies arrived on the run, with their guns out.

"Where the hell have *you* two been?" the sheriff demanded. "You're a little late."

"We was at the other end of town, Quake," one of the deputies said.

"Yeah," the other said, "doin' rounds."

"Yeah," the sheriff, Earthquake Nolan, said,

"you was goin' round and round with a couple of Miss Lottie's whores, that's what you were doin'."

"Sheriff," Sherry Lance said, "*when* are you going to get a posse together?"

"As soon as I can, Miss Lance," Earthquake said. He pointed down at the dead man on the floor, who everyone seemed to have forgotten, and said, "First I got to take care of Mr. Royce."

Royce was one of the tellers, and while he hadn't exactly made a *menacing* move at the bank robbers, he *had* moved, and one of them had shot him dead.

"He's *dead,*" Sherry said. "What can you do for him?"

Earthquake turned to his deputies and said, "Take Mr. Royce's body over to the undertaker's."

"Right, Quake," Randy Russell said. He was Earthquake's first deputy, a tall, slender man with a mustache and some chin hair just under his lip. He left the rest of his jaw clean.

"And Randy," Earthquake said, "after that round up some men for a posse."

"Right, Quake," Russell said. He turned to Pardee Hall, the second deputy, and said, "Let's go, Pardee."

Together they lifted Mr. Royce and carried him from the bank.

"Sheriff—"

"Miss Lance, *please,*" Earthquake said, and Sherry fell into a resentful silence.

Earthquake looked at Mr. Devine, the bank manager, and said, "I need to have the men described, Mr. Devine."

"All I saw," Devine said, "was a big gun." He stuck his jaw out then, as if daring the sheriff to criticize him.

"Were they wearing masks?" the sheriff asked.

"No."

"How many of them spoke?"

"Just one," Devine said, "the one holding the gun on me."

"And what did *he* look like?"

Mr. Devine flapped his arms helplessly and said, "Uh, a man with a gun."

Earthquake knew this wasn't going to be easy. The robbers *weren't* wearing masks and yet they *still* couldn't be described. They probably knew that everyone would be too scared to take a good look at them. *Not* wearing masks, in this instance, was a smart thing to do.

"I can identify one of them," Edwina Rawlins said, stepping forward. Edwina was the other teller, a spinster in her fifties, probably the most mean-spirited woman in town. She reveled in the fact that she handled everyone *else's* money.

"Miss Rawlins," Earthquake said. "You can identify the bank robbers?"

"Just one of them," she said. "I recognized him right off, and I'm surprised no one else did."

"Well . . . who was it?"

She drew herself up to her full five foot two and said, "Will Spenser."

Earthquake stared at her and said, "*Young* Will Spenser?"

"Young indeed," she said. "He's old enough to rob a bank and point a gun at *me*."

"Are you sure about this, Miss Rawlins?" Earthquake asked.

"I am *not* blind, Sheriff!"

"I never said you was, ma'am."

"As a matter of fact," Betty Prince said, "I think I remember seeing young Spenser also."

Mrs. Prince was the wife of Harold Prince, who owned the general store. She was there making a deposit for her husband.

"Are *you* sure, Mrs. Prince?" the sheriff asked.

"Uh . . . yes, I believe I am sure, Sheriff."

"I'm sure too," Devine said.

"Mr. Devine," Earthquake said, "I thought all *you* could see was a gun."

"Well . . . Will Spenser's yellow hair is kind of hard to miss, don't you think?"

"Indeed!" Miss Rawlins said huffily.

Earthquake looked at Miss Rawlins, Mrs. Prince, and Mr. Devine, took a deep breath, and then said, "All right, I'll start lookin' for Will Spenser."

SIX

Clint was in a foul mood.

In his own mind he had already been *out* of Broken Back, Kansas. Now, through no fault of his own, he was going to be stuck there two—or *three*—weeks. Luckily, he'd gotten the liveryman to split the cost of the new wheel down the middle. He'd wanted the man to pay for the whole thing, but *that* argument could have gone *on* for two or three weeks.

From the livery he went to the saloon. There, sitting at a table over a beer, he heard all of the stories that were circulating about the bank robbery.

" . . . fifteen bank robbers . . ."

" . . . Earthquake took them on single-handed . . ."

" . . . I ain't ridin' on no posse . . ."

" . . . Tom Connor is gonna be *mad* as a wet cat . . ."

" . . . Will Spenser was the leader . . ."

" . . . Jeannie Spenser says it can't be, not *her* boy . . ."

" . . . there's witnesses . . ."

It was all very sketchy, but he thought he was able to put it together. Apparently, a young man from the town, Will Spenser, was being accused of being one of the bank robbers, and his mother was denying it. The sheriff—whose name was *Earthquake*?—was trying to put a posse together, but word was spreading that there were twice as many—or even *three* times as many—robbers as there actually were, and he wasn't getting very many takers.

Clint was getting no credit for being part of the gun battle that afternoon—which was just as well—and Tom Connor seemed to be the owner of the bank.

Clint had had prior dealings with bank owners who took robberies personally, and he didn't *like* dealing with them. Even though he was stuck in Broken Back, he was determined to stay out of the bank robbery matter.

Of course, that wasn't going to be easy.

First, the sheriff came to him. He was still sitting in the saloon when the man's massive bulk filled the doorway. It was no surprise that the sheriff was called "Earthquake." Clint just wondered if that was the name his parents had given him.

Sheriff Earthquake—as Clint had come to think of him—scanned the room, spotted Clint, and lumbered over to him. He scattered men before him, and left them staggering in his wake.

"Mr. Adams," he said politely. "Can I sit?"

"Sure, Sheriff," Clint said, and then thought, *If you can find a chair that will hold you.*

The man pulled out a chair and lowered himself into it carefully. It groaned in protest, but held.

"A beer?" Clint asked.

"Why not?" Earthquake said, rubbing a massive paw over his bearded face. He took off his hat, setting it down on the table. What hair he had was dark, but his scalp was easily visible through it.

"I'll get it," Clint said. He didn't want to take the chance of the sheriff getting up, and then sitting down again in the same chair. The second time, it might not hold.

Clint went to the bar, got the sheriff's beer, and brought it back to him, then sat back down opposite him.

"What can I do for you?"

"I wanted to thank you for trying to help me this afternoon," Earthquake said.

"That's okay," Clint said. "I have to admit it was against my better judgment."

"Well, I know who you are," Earthquake said, "and you probably saved my butt by taking a hand. Thanks."

"No problem," Clint said. "Was that all?"

"No," Earthquake said. He took a moment to take a sip of beer—and half the contents of the mug disappeared! He wiped his mouth with the back of his hand.

"No, that's not all," he continued. "I need your help. I'm having trouble getting up a posse."

"So I've heard," Clint said.

Earthquake looked around and said, "It's their money, but *they* won't do anything to try and get it back."

"Why should they?" Clint said. "It's *your* job." The sheriff gave him a look and Clint hurriedly added, "That's, uh, the way *they're* thinking, of course."

"Sure," Earthquake said, "I *know* it's my job, but it's *still* their money. You'd think they'd want to help."

"You'd think so," Clint said, "but it never quite works out that way. See, when you put on that badge everybody in town figures that it's your responsibility to take care of anything bad that happens. You take the job, you appoint a couple of deputies, and that's it." Clint made a motion as if he was washing his hands. "They did their part, and now it's up to you."

Earthquake used his thumb and forefinger to wipe the corners of his mouth.

"I'm not real good at this, you know," he said finally. "I got the job because of my size. People figured I could keep the drunks in line, you know? Who expected somebody to rob the goddamned bank of Broken Back."

"How long are you in the job?"

"Just a coupla months."

Clint looked at the man and said, "Maybe somebody *did* expect it."

Earthquake stared across the table at Clint and said, "Are you sayin' that I was voted into this job because somebody was already plannin' to rob the bank?"

"Maybe."

"But . . . the town voted," Earthquake said. "The whole *town* couldn't be in on it."

"They wouldn't have to be," Clint said. "Just the people who count the votes."

"You mean . . . the election was fixed because they figured they could rob the bank with me as sheriff and get away with it?"

Clint waved one hand in the air and said, "We're just discussing possibilities, Sheriff."

"Well," Earthquake said, "I can tell you one thing. They *ain't* gonna get away with it. Not by a long sight. Not if I got to chase them down myself single-handed."

"You've got two deputies," Clint reminded him.

Earthquake leaned forward and said, "I'd do a lot better if you'd join up with me."

Clint shook his head and said, "Ah, I don't think so, Sheriff. It's really not my business, you know? If it wasn't for the fact that my wagon needs repairing, I wouldn't even be here."

"I wish I could convince you," Earthquake said.

"I'm sorry," Clint said, shaking his head emphatically. "The answer is no."

Earthquake looked at a loss for words for a moment, then stood up from his chair, said, "Sorry I bothered you," and left the saloon.

SEVEN

Clint was still sitting in the saloon, nursing a second beer and trying to decide whether or not to join a poker game that had started up at another table, when the batwing doors opened again and a woman stepped in. She attracted attention, both because she was a woman, and because she was a *handsome* woman. She was blond, tall, and slender, in her forties but wearing it *very* well.

She stood just inside the doors looking around the room, obviously looking for someone in particular.

"Hey," a man at a nearby table called out drunkenly, "I'm over here, honey."

She ignored him, and he didn't like it. He got up and walked over to her.

"Hey, honey—" he started, but she made an impatient gesture towards him, waving her hand as if he were just an annoyance.

"I said *hey,*" he said, and grabbed her by the arm. By the look on her face he was squeezing it pretty hard.

"Shit," Clint said under his breath, for two reasons. Number one, he was compelled to step in and help her, and number two, he had the uncomfortable feeling that she was looking for him to begin with.

"That's it, cowboy," he said, taking hold of the man's free arm. "The lady's with me."

"Oh, yeah?" the man said, eyeing Clint drunkenly. Clint didn't have much to worry about. He had one of the man's arms, and the other was holding the *woman's* arm.

"Yeah," Clint said. He slid his hand down the man's arm until he was holding his wrist. He squeezed, feeling the fragile wrist bones begin to grind together. "Let her go, friend."

"Ow, Jesus—" the man yelped. He released the woman's arm and tried to pull free of Clint's hold.

Before releasing him Clint looked over at the table where the man had been sitting with some friends.

"One of you want to come over here and keep your friend from doing anything foolish when I let him go?"

One of them got up nervously and came over. Clint released the man's arm then and took the woman's hand.

"Come on," he said to her. "Come and sit over here."

She resisted.

"Are you Mister Adams?"

"That's right," Clint said.

"I'm looking for you then," she said.

"I was afraid of that," he said. He tugged her hand again and said, "Come on."

Behind them he could hear the second man talking to the first man, trying to get him back to the table.

"Who does he think he is?" the first man demanded.

"The man who could have crushed your wrist if he wanted to," the second man said. "Come *on*!"

Clint held the chair for the woman as she sat. It was the same chair the sheriff had been in, and it accommodated her with much more ease.

"Can I get you a drink?" he asked.

"No, thank you."

He nodded and sat down opposite her.

"My name is Jeannie Spenser, Mr. Adams," she said. "My son is Will Spenser."

He nodded and picked up his beer.

"They say my son Will was with the bank robbers this afternoon."

"I've heard that, Mrs. Spenser."

"Well, he couldn't have been."

"There were witnesses, ma'am," he said.

"Witnesses," she said, the word rolling with distaste off her tongue. "Mrs. Rawlins, that old busybody."

"Still—"

"Well, even if he *was* with them," she said, "it couldn't have been of his own accord."

"I wouldn't know that, Mrs. Spenser."

"Well, I would," she said. "Will's a good boy, Mr. Adams."

Everybody's boy is a good boy, he thought, but he didn't say it.

"Mrs. Spenser," he said, "the sheriff will be riding out after the robbers very shortly. If your son needs help—"

"The sheriff thinks he was one of the robbers," she said. "He came and asked me about Will. Who his friends were, and all."

"And did you tell him?"

"Tell him what?" she asked. "I don't know who Will's friends are—or were."

"How old is your son, Mrs. Spenser?"

"Eighteen."

"Old enough to make his own friends," Clint said, "and his own decisions."

She glared at him and said, "You think he was in on it too?"

He spread his hands in a helpless gesture and said, "I don't know anything about it, Mrs. Spenser."

"You were there," she said. "You were trying to stop them."

"Yes, I was."

"Trying to help."

"Yes."

"Then I want you to try to help me."

"Mrs. Spenser—"

"I want you to find my son and prove that he *wasn't* one of the bank robbers."

"Mrs. Spenser," Clint said patiently, "that certainly isn't my job."

"I *know* it isn't your job," she said. "I'm *asking* for your help."

"I'm afraid I can't give it, ma'am," he said. "I just don't want to get involved."

"I don't understand," she said, sitting back in her chair. "How can you *not* help?"

"Mrs. Spenser—"

"You're as bad as the rest of them," she said accusingly. She stood up, almost knocking the chair over behind her.

"Mrs. Spenser, I'm sure the sheriff will do his best—" he began, but she was having none of it.

"I don't need your advice, Mr. Adams, or your assurances," she said, cutting him off. "If you won't help me, I'll find someone who will."

She turned and stormed out of the saloon.

Clint had started to rise, and now settled back in his chair, looking around. He was the center of attention, at least for a moment. The drunk whose wrist he had damaged was looking over at him with a satisfied look on his face.

"Didn't do no better than me, did you?" the man said.

"I guess not," Clint said, and lifted his beer.

EIGHT

Clint had finally decided to join the poker game and, after two hours of play, was doing quite well for himself when Sherry Lance entered the saloon. Tall, dark-haired, and full-bodied, she put every saloon girl in the place to shame, and they knew it. While the men were casting admiring glances her way, the saloon girls were looking daggers at her. If looks could kill, she would have been dead ten times over.

She looked the place over, finally spotted Clint, and stalked over to where he was sitting.

"Here you are," she said.

"Where am I supposed to be?"

"I *thought* you'd be talking with the sheriff."

"We did that earlier."

"So," she asked, "are you going out with the posse?"

"No."

"Why not?"

"It's not my business, Sherry."

"I *told* you that my *money* was in the bank," she said. "Didn't you hear me?"

Why had he not noticed before what a shrew she was? Maybe it was because all they had done for the past week was give each other what they wanted. Now that he *wasn't* going to give her what she wanted, her attitude was rapidly becoming annoying. Did she think that a few days in bed together meant he had to risk *his* life for *her* money?

"Sherry," he said, looking up at her, "there are probably a dozen men in this place who would join that posse if you smiled at them. Why not try it?"

"Because I don't want *them,* Clint," she said, suddenly pouty. "I want you." She stamped her foot for emphasis.

"I can't do it, Sherry," he said. "I'm sorry, but this time I'm staying out of it."

She glared at him for a few moments, then said, "Ooooh," with feeling and stalked out.

The saloon girls, seeing that Sherry and Clint were *not* exactly getting along, started paying him special attention again, as they had the first night.

The drunk whose wrist Clint had previously bruised obviously liked seeing women walk out on him. The man got up and walked over to the table.

"Not having much luck with women tonight, are you, mister?"

"I guess not," Clint said, looking to avoid trouble—especially while he was holding such a good hand.

"No, siree," the man said, "walkin' out on you, they are." He laughed, finding it much funnier than anyone else in the place.

Clint looked up at the man and said coldly, "Why don't you go back to your friends?"

The man ignored the comment.

"You any better at cards than you are at women, mister?" he asked. "I bet you ain't. Whataya got there, huh?"

The man leaned over, trying to see Clint's cards and blowing his fetid breath in Clint's face. Clint stiff-armed him, driving him several feet backwards.

"Hey!" the man said. "You lookin' for trouble?" He took a few steps until he was close to the poker table again.

"I'm looking to *avoid* trouble," Clint said. He looked past the man at his friends and said, "Somebody come and get this—"

"Don't be lookin' at them!" the drunk said. "They ain't gonna help this time. It's just you and me. Now . . . you apologize."

"For what?" Clint asked.

The man started to speak, then stopped. Obviously, he hadn't quite figured *that* part out yet.

"Go away," Clint said.

"Don't turn away from me," the drunk said, and made a move for his gun.

Clint moved quickly. He flicked out one leg

and swept both of the drunk's legs out from under him with a sweeping move. The man shouted, fell backward, hit his head on the floor, and was knocked cold.

Clint looked over at the other table and said, "*Now* come and get him, and get him *out* of here."

There were three men at the table and they all got up and hurried over. They lifted their unconscious friend and carried him from the saloon.

"All right," Clint said, "before somebody else comes in, whose play is it?"

NINE

Sheriff Earthquake Nolan dragged his ass back into town at the end of the third day after the robbery. Clint didn't know how the sheriff expected to find anybody by going out in the morning and coming back at night. All he could do was go over the same ground again and again. Of course, maybe if he'd had himself a posse, he might have gone out and stayed out long enough to get the job done.

During the three days Clint ran into Sherry Lance a couple of times, but each time she looked the other way. That suited him. She was good in bed, but she put too high a price on it for him.

In his desperate loneliness he had turned to a saloon girl named Rose—Rosetta was her real name, but she didn't like it, and he refused to call her by that name anyway. Rose was short, full-bodied, and enthusiastic. All she wanted from him was to make her feel as good as she made him feel. That was the kind of price he could handle.

So the first night she was sitting astride him, riding him for all she was worth. Her fleshy breasts bounced as *she* bounced up and down on him, and he finally reached up and held them, popping the nipples between his fingers. She made that high-pitched sound deep in her throat that she made just before the loud one, the scream that came when she was going to come. He pulled her down to him and kissed her, successfully muffling the sound of the scream . . .

He walked to the window while she slept. It was her day off in the saloon, and they had spent most of the late afternoon and early evening in bed together. That was why he was standing at the window when Sheriff Earthquake came riding in. His horse, a big bay mare, had her head down and was practically dragging her ass. It must have been a tough job, toting Earthquake Nolan around all day long.

Clint decided to let Rose sleep for a while. He got dressed and went out to get a beer. His knees felt weak, which wasn't hard to understand after hours in bed with little Rose.

He went to the Broken Back Saloon, and found an open spot at the bar. The bartender's name was Ray, and he had come to know Clint as a regular since Clint had started seeing Rose.

"Beer?" Ray asked.

"A nice cold one."

Ray drew the beer and set it down in front of Clint.

"What'd you do to Rose?" the bartender asked.

"She's asleep."

"I didn't know she slept," Ray said, smiling. Someone at the other end of the bar called him and he hurried down there.

Clint held the beer mug in his hand and turned to take a look at the room. There was a poker game going, not the same one he'd sat in on earlier in the week. That one had broken up, probably because Clint was the only one winning anything. He watched this game for a while, and decided he didn't want any part of it. There was a slick dresser in the game who dealt even slicker than he dressed.

"Hear about Connor?"

The question came from behind him. He turned and saw that Ray was back.

"Connor?"

"Tom Connor, guy who owns the bank."

"Oh, him," Clint said. "What about him?"

"Came to town today," Ray said. "Had it out with the town council. If Quake didn't come back with the money today, Connor said he was bringin' in his own people."

"Who?"

"Got me," Ray said. "He wants the town to pay for it, though."

"Will they?"

"Doubt it. Connor will probably have to go into his own pocket—or the bank's."

"In which case," Clint observed, "the town ends up paying for it anyway."

That startled Ray, as he hadn't thought of it that way before.

"You know," he said, "I got money in the bank—or I did anyway. Maybe I'll take it out—whenever they get it back, that is."

"Sounds like a good idea to me," Clint said. He sipped his beer and added, "I just saw the sheriff riding back in."

"Empty-handed, I guess."

"Yep."

"I don't think he's gonna have that job much longer, Clint," Ray said.

"That's not fair," Clint said. "He was right on the spot the day of the robbery. He had no backup."

"Nobody's gonna remember that," Ray said. "All they're gonna remember is that he let the bank get robbed, didn't catch the robbers, and didn't get the money back."

"Not fair," Clint said again, but he knew the bartender was right.

Ray went off to tend bar again, and Clint leaned his elbows on the bar. His half-finished beer was just below his chin.

He was bored. He debated with himself. Stay and finish the beer, and maybe have another, or go and talk with Earthquake?

He ignored the half-finished beer on the bar and left the saloon.

TEN

Clint walked to the sheriff's office. The worn-out bay mare was out front, and her head was still hanging almost to the ground. She gave him a baleful stare as he went by, and he simply shrugged.

He mounted the boardwalk and knocked on the door.

"Come on in," Earthquake Nolan called.

Clint entered, and saw the big man sitting behind his desk. He was hangdog tired, like the horse out front, and could barely lift his eyes to look at his visitor.

"What can I do for you, Mr. Adams?"

Clint didn't know how to answer that. What *could* Nolan do for him? Talk to him? Tell him a story so he wouldn't be so bored?

"I was just wondering how the . . . the hunt was

going?" Clint asked lamely.

Earthquake waved a big paw, telling Clint to come closer. Then he pointed to the back, where the cells were.

"See anybody in those cells?" he asked. "That's how the hunt is goin'."

"Not good, huh?"

"Not a sniff," Earthquake said. "Of course, there's the fact that I just ain't good at this, and the fact that I ain't got a posse, *or* a goddamned deputy I can count on. I guess that means it ain't all my fault—'ceptin' I'm the sheriff, so it is." He squinted at Clint and asked, "Ain't that the way of it when you're wearin' a badge?"

"I guess it is," Clint said.

"Got coffee over there," Earthquake said. "From this morning, but it's hot. Help yerself."

Clint went over to the stove and poured some of the vile-smelling liquid into a cup.

"Some for you?" he asked.

"Take more'n coffee to perk me up," the big man said.

"Why don't you get some sleep?"

"I go to sleep I'll likely wake up without a job," the sheriff said. "Tom Connor was comin' into town this mornin' when I left."

"I heard."

"You also hear he's thinkin' of bringin' in his own people?"

"Heard that too."

Earthquake raised his chin up off his chest for the first time and asked, "You hear who?"

"No," Clint admitted, "I didn't hear that."

Earthquake hesitated a moment, then said, "Lloyd Kennedy and his bunch."

Clint stared at Earthquake and put his coffee cup down on the man's desk.

"Captain Vigilante?"

Earthquake frowned and asked, "Who calls him that? I never heard it before."

"*I* call him that."

"It fits," the man said. "You don't like him, do you?"

"No," Clint said, surprising himself. "I don't know the man, but he's probably the *only* man I don't know and *still* don't like."

"He gets the job done."

"So does a bounty hunter," Clint said.

"Same scum."

"I know some bounty hunters who I respect," Clint said. "I don't think I'd ever come to respect Kennedy. Of course, there's always the possibility that I'm judging him unfairly based on his reputation. Lord knows, that's been done to *me* long enough, but even with that . . ." He finished up by shaking his head. "I guess I should give him a fair shake, but I've heard stories from people I know, stories that are *more* than rumors."

"What kind of stories?"

Still shaking his head, Clint said, "Kennedy . . . he's just a vicious animal who likes to get paid for hurting people, and for killing them."

"And the men he runs?"

"Like him," Clint said.

"Know any of them?"

"Some," Clint said, then amended it to, "One. Soc Valdez."

"Soc?"

"Socrates," Clint said.

"What?"

"It's Greek," Clint said. "He had a Mexican father who read Greek philosophy."

"Greek what?"

"Never mind," Clint said. "Soc is the only man who rides with Kennedy who I've ever met, and he's a killer, pure and simple. I think Henny O'Day used to ride with Kennedy. I never met him, but I know his work."

"The way I hear it he runs about five men these days," Earthquake said. "Connor is gonna dangle enough money in front of Kennedy to get him to Broken Back, and then he'll turn him loose on that Spenser kid."

Clint frowned. "Why the kid?"

"He's the only one of the bunch who wasn't a pro," Earthquake said.

"That makes sense," Clint said, nodding. "He'd leave the biggest trail."

"Right," Earthquake said. Now it was his turn shake his head. "Jesus, if Kennedy catches up with that kid . . . whether he's guilty or not . . ."

"You still have some doubts?" Clint asked.

"His momma is sure convinced he couldn't have been involved," Earthquake said, then added with a shrug, "Course, that's his momma."

Clint made a point of not picking up the coffee

cup again. He drank almost anything that disguised itself as coffee, but he found this brew just *too* foreign . . .

"Well," he said, moving towards the door, "just thought I'd stop in and . . . see how things were . . ."

Earthquake lifted a hand in a silent farewell.

As Clint opened the door to leave, though, the big man said, "Jesus, if Kennedy catches that kid . . ."

Clint closed the door on the man's words, but not on his own thoughts.

ELEVEN

Tom Connor frowned at the members of the town council. It was the morning of the fourth day after the robbery. Connor was trying one more time to get the council to foot the bill for the services of Lloyd Kennedy and his vigilantes.

"Tom," Ben Griffith, the mayor of Broken Back, said, "we're responsible for the sheriff's salary, and that of his deputies. There are no provisions for paying vigilantes."

"Then fire the sheriff and his deputies," Connor said, "and use the money to pay Kennedy and his men."

Griffith did not even consider the suggestion. "For one thing," he said, "the salaries of a sheriff and two deputies would hardly pay this man Kennedy. No, I think you're going to have to foot the bill for this one, Tom."

Connor looked directly at Griffith, ignoring the other five members of the council. He knew that Griffith, fifty-five and one of the original citizens of Broken Back, was his opposition. The others would go whichever way Griffith wanted them to go.

"My bank means a lot to this town, Ben," he said warningly.

Griffith smiled and said, "We existed for a long time without a bank, Tom. If you know anything about me, you know I don't react well to threats."

Connor glared at Griffith, then turned and left the council room.

Collectively, the other members of the council let out a sigh.

"You're taking a big chance, Ben," Dean Lewis said. He was the owner of the hardware store.

"With *our* futures," Harold Prince, the owner of the general store, said.

"You gentlemen are free to vote on this," Griffith said to Lewis, Prince, and the others. "If you want to allot money for vigilantes, then vote on it. I vote no."

"Don't get testy, Ben," Judge Marshall Holder said. Holder was the only member of the council older than Griffith. In fact, the two men had *started* the town council years ago. "Nobody is going against you."

"It's not a matter of going against me, Marshall," Griffith said. "It's a matter of doing what's right for the town."

"Losing our bank?" Prince asked. "That's right for the town?"

"We'd open another bank, Harold," Griffith said. "Maybe even do it ourselves. A citizens' bank."

"Sure," Lewis said. "we don't have money to pay a bounty hunter, but we're gonna open our own bank."

"Lloyd Kennedy is a little more than a bounty hunter, gentlemen," Judge Holder said. "Believe me, I've dealt with men like him before. If he was *only* a bounty hunter . . ."

"Well, we need someone," Lewis said, cutting the judge off. "Earthquake sure ain't doin' the job."

"We knew when we elected Earthquake that he'd be an adequate sheriff at best," Griffith said. "In fact, I think he's been better than that."

"I agree," Holder said.

Lewis stood up and said, "If we don't get that money back, or if Connor pulls out, I'm gonna want Earthquake's head on a plate."

Prince stood and said, "So will I," and both men left.

The other two members of the council stood up and left quietly.

Griffith and Holder exchanged glances, and then Holder said, "They're the future, Ben."

Griffith shook his head, laughed without humor, and said, "God help Broken Back."

Tom Connor went from the town hall directly to the bank. As he walked past Walter Devine's desk he said, "As soon as Lloyd Kennedy gets here, send him right into my office."

"Yes, sir," Devine said.

The bank manager had always had eyes for Connor's office, and wondered peevishly why he couldn't use it when the man wasn't there.

Connor went into his office and sat behind his desk. He wasn't disappointed that the council wouldn't allot funds for Kennedy and his men. He hadn't really expected it, but he'd *had* to try. It was just as well that the depositors would be footing the bill. Not only the depositors of this bank, but all the others that he owned.

He'd used Lloyd Kennedy before, and Kennedy knew that he wanted results. He also knew he'd be paid well for them. And *this* job was easier because they knew who one of the robbers was, that young Will Spenser. It was too bad. Connor remembered that Jeannie Spenser was a good-looking woman. Still, her son was a criminal and he was going to pay for robbing one of Tom Connor's banks. He would pay *heavily* when Lloyd Kennedy caught up to him.

Connor sat back in his chair and made a mental note to fire Devine when this was all over.

TWELVE

Clint Adams was sitting out in front of the cafe later that afternoon when Lloyd Kennedy and his boys rode into town. They attracted attention because they looked like what they were, a bunch of killers.

Clint knew who they were because he recognized Soc Valdez. The man had to be about thirty-seven or eight now, but he looked the same as he had the last time Clint had seen him. That must have been five or six years ago. Valdez had a squat powerful body that made him look shorter than he really was, especially when he was on a horse. When he stepped down, men were often surprised to find themselves looking *up* at Socrates Valdez.

As the group of six rode past Clint he examined the man in the lead. He assumed this was Lloyd

Kennedy. Kennedy had been an officer during the Civil War, and he sat his horse like one. He sat up very straight, his back erect, his chin high, and he *looked* like a man in command. Clint had never seen him before, and was surprised at the apparent youth of the man. For someone who was an officer during the war, he looked barely forty, and Clint knew he had to be at least fifty.

Although Kennedy did not turn his head to look at him, Clint had a feeling he was being studied. On the other hand, Soc Valdez looked directly at him, and Clint could see the recognition dawn on the man's face. They nodded to each other, with no expression revealed on their faces.

Clint watched as the six men rode to the bank and stopped out front. They all dismounted, but it was only Kennedy who went in. Just before he did, though, he saw a brief exchange pass between Kennedy and Valdez . . .

"Who was that man, Soc?" Kennedy asked.

"Clint Adams, Boss," Valdez said. In private Valdez called Kennedy by his first name. In public, or even around the other men, he called him "Boss."

"The Gunsmith?" Kennedy asked. "*That* Clint Adams?"

"The one and only, Boss."

"I wonder what he's doing here."

"He travels around a lot," Valdez said. "Never stays in one place too long that I know of."

"Well," Kennedy said, "it would be nice to know if he's involved in this."

Valdez nodded and said, "See what I can do, Boss."

Kennedy went into the bank and presented himself to Devine, the manager.

"Can I help you?" Devine asked.

"Lloyd Kennedy."

"Oh, yes, Mr. Kennedy," Devine said. He stated to rise, hesitated, then continued, saying, "I'll tell Mr. Connor you're here."

"Don't bother," Kennedy said. "Just point the way."

Still not totally erect, Devine paused again, then just pointed to Connor's office.

"Thanks," Kennedy said, and walked to the open office door. He entered without knocking, and Connor looked up from his desk in surprise.

"You could have knocked," he said, annoyed.

"You're right, Tom," Kennedy said, "I could have."

Kennedy walked to the empty chair in front of Connor's desk and sat down.

"Do I need to know anything other than what was in your telegram?" Kennedy asked.

"You might want to talk to the mother," Connor said, "and my employees. Other than that, you've got it all."

"I'll talk to the sheriff too," Kennedy said, smiling tightly. He had a small mouth, and barely moved his lips when he spoke. "Pay my respects," he added.

"Ha," Connor said, "from what I understand he doesn't *deserve* your respect."

"And you do?" Kennedy asked.

"Lloyd—"

"Your money does, Tom," Kennedy went on. "I respect money, you know that, but don't try to tell me when I should or shouldn't respect a man."

"Just get the job done, Lloyd," Tom said. "I don't care who or what you respect as long as you get it done."

Kennedy stood up. "My men and I will be at the hotel," he said. "I'll talk to the people I have to talk to, and we'll probably head out early."

"Good."

Kennedy nodded and left the office. Instead of stopping to talk to Devine and the other employees, he went directly outside.

"Soc," he said, "have somebody take the horses to the livery, and have somebody register us at the hotel. Three rooms, one for me, one for you, and one room for the others."

These instructions were always the same, and yet Kennedy always gave them as if it was the first time.

"Right, Boss."

"I'm gonna talk to the people in the bank," he said. "When you're settled, come back. You and I are gonna talk to the boy's mother."

"Right."

"And Soc," Kennedy said, "find out about Adams."

"I will."

Kennedy nodded, turned, and went back into the bank.

Clint watched as Kennedy went back into the bank and the other men slowly dispersed. Two of them took the horses to the livery, and the other three walked over to the hotel. Clint saw Valdez looked over towards him, but the man made no move to approach him.

Not yet anyway.

THIRTEEN

Clint knew if he stayed where he was Soc Valdez would get to him. It was inevitable. Both he and Kennedy would have to be wondering what he was doing in Broken Back, Kansas. They would also have to know if he had any intention of taking a hand in their business.

So he waited.

He didn't have long to wait. When Valdez came out of the hotel with two of Kennedy's other men, they split up. The two men went towards the saloon, while Valdez turned and walked towards Clint. Clint thought he recognized one of the two men as Henny O'Day, but he wasn't sure.

Clint could smell dinner cooking inside the cafe. He'd started eating there instead of the hotel because the food was a hell of a lot better. In about an hour he'd go in and eat—that is, unless Soc Valdez succeeded in ruining his appetite.

He watched as the man crossed the street and walked towards him. Valdez still had a droopy mustache and a bit of hair beneath his lower lip. His eyes were heavy-lidded, but Clint knew that was natural and not from fatigue.

Valdez mounted the boardwalk and Clint sat back in his chair, pressing his back against the wall. Soc Valdez was the last man in the world he would have wanted to give his back to.

Finally the man reached him and stopped.

"Adams," he said, with a nod.

"Hello, Soc."

"What are you doin' in this town?"

Valdez still spoke with just a touch of a Mexican accent.

"Get right to it, why don't you?" Clint asked.

"You have anything to do with the bank robbery?" Valdez asked.

"I didn't do it, if that's what you mean."

"I think you know what I mean."

"Your boss wants to know what I'm doing here, right?" Clint asked.

Valdez didn't answer, and suddenly Clint wasn't in such a cooperative mood. It would have been so easy just to say that it was pure coincidence that he happened to be in town when the bank was robbed, but that was not what he said.

"I tell you what," he said instead. "If your boss is so interested, tell him to come and ask me himself."

"He don't have time for that," Valdez said.

"Tell him to make time," Clint said.

Valdez frowned and asked, "Why you bein' hard about this?"

"Maybe because I don't like your boss."

"You don't know 'im."

"So," Clint said, "let him come and introduce himself, and change my mind."

Valdez stood his ground for a few moments, then said, "I'll tell him."

"You do that," Clint said. "Good to see you, Soc. You look the same."

"So do you," Valdez said. With that he turned and walked away.

Clint wasn't sure if he wanted to eat now so his meal wouldn't be interrupted, or just wait.

Valdez went right from talking to Clint Adams to the bank. Lloyd Kennedy was coming out as he got there.

"Good timing," Kennedy said. "These assholes don't know anything but that they recognized the kid."

"The mother's next, then," Valdez said.

"Right," Kennedy said. He looked over to where Clint Adams was sitting, and then looked at Valdez. "You talk to Adams?"

"Tried."

"Not cooperative?"

"No."

"Why not?"

"He don't like you."

"He don't know me."

Valdez shrugged.

"You know him well?"

"I know him," Valdez said, "but not well."

"Should I go and talk to him?"

"I would, Lloyd," Valdez said, "if I was you."

"Why?"

"Because right now he is a wild card," Valdez said. "We don't know why he's here or what he has to do with anything."

"He may have *nothing* to do with anything," Kennedy said.

"But until we know that for sure," Valdez said, "he's still a wild card—and right now he won't talk to nobody but you."

Kennedy looked over at Clint Adams again.

"All right," he said finally. "We'll talk to the mother, and then I'll have a talk with Clint Adams. Hell, maybe I'll even buy him dinner. Maybe that'll make him like me."

Valdez didn't smile when he said, "I think it will take more than that."

FOURTEEN

When Jean Spenser saw the two men on her doorstep she became frightened. Still, she went to the door and opened it and, with her chin held high, asked, "Yes, can I help you? Would you like a room?"

Kennedy didn't know what Jean Spenser meant at first, but then he realized that she ran a rooming house. If it became necessary to pressure her, he could always simply take a room.

"Mrs. Spenser?"

"That's right."

"My name is Lloyd Kennedy, ma'am," he said. "This is my associate, Mr. Valdez."

"You're the bounty hunter," she said.

"I don't call it that," he said.

"Call it what you like," she said, "that's what it is."

"Can we come in?"

"No," she said, and stepped outside. "We can talk out here."

Kennedy found himself liking her. He sensed that she was afraid, but otherwise she didn't show it, and she wasn't afraid to speak up—*and* she was a handsome woman. Suddenly, Kennedy was sorry that he had little time for women who weren't whores.

"I've been hired by the bank to find the bank robbers, Mrs. Spenser," he said. "I understand your son was one of them."

"I don't believe that."

"I can understand that," Kennedy said, "but you must also understand that I have to go by what witnesses have told me. Your son was identified as one of the bank robbers. I have to ask you if you can help me find him."

She folded her arms firmly in front of her and glared at him.

"Even if I did believe that he was one of the bank robbers, I wouldn't help *you* find him," she said. "You only want to kill him."

"That's not true, ma'am."

"I know your reputation, Mr. Kennedy."

He smiled a disarming smile and said, "Reputations are overrated."

There was more about him that was disarming than just his smile. He didn't *seem* like a bounty hunter, or a vicious killer. In fact, he was so well mannered it totally threw her off balance.

"There's nothing I can tell you to help you find

my son, Mr. Kennedy," she said. "I simply don't know where he is."

"Do you know where he'd go if he was in trouble?" Kennedy asked. "To his father perhaps?"

She hesitated, then said, "His father is dead. No, there's nothing I can tell you that will help you."

Now Kennedy hesitated, and then said, "All right, ma'am. I'm sorry I bothered you. Come on, Soc."

As Valdez and Kennedy stepped down from the porch Jean Spenser said, "Mr. Kennedy?"

"Yes?" he turned and looked up at her.

"Don't kill my son," she said. "I'm warning you. Do what you want to those bank robbers, but don't kill my son."

"I don't want to kill your son, Mrs. Spenser," Kennedy said, "but I have a job to do, and I'm going to do it. Good day."

Jean Spenser stood on the porch and watched the two men walk away. She stayed there until they were out of sight, rubbing her arms as if she was cold, and then she turned and went back inside.

"You gave up easy," Valdez said.

"No," Kennedy said, "I didn't."

"We didn't find out anything."

"Yes, we did."

"What?" Valdez said. "I didn't hear nothing."

Kennedy looked at Valdez and said, "You've got to listen with more than just your ears, Soc. You have to listen with your eyes too."

Valdez grew annoyed. He hated when Kennedy talked to him like that.

"You know I don't understand things like that," Valdez said. "Tell me."

"The boy's father."

"What about him?" Valdez said. "She said he's dead."

Now Kennedy smiled and said, "She lied."

FIFTEEN

Walking back from Jean Spenser's rooming house, Kennedy decided to go and see the sheriff before seeing Clint Adams. While he had very little respect for the law, he recognized the importance of making small concessions to it—such as paying his *respects* to the local law.

"Wait outside," he told Valdez when they reached the sheriff's office.

"Why?"

"Because I know how you and lawmen get along," Kennedy said.

Valdez frowned and said, "We don't."

"Exactly," Kennedy said, and went inside.

Valdez stepped down off the boardwalk, and while rolling a cigarette looked over to where Clint Adams had been sitting earlier. Clint wasn't there anymore. He had probably gone inside the cafe to eat. Valdez wondered idly if Kennedy was going to let him go inside the cafe with him. If not, he'd just go over to the saloon with the other boys.

He lit the cigarette, and wondered where the local whorehouse was.

As Kennedy entered the office he was surprised at the man seated behind the desk. The sheer size of the man was astounding.

"Can I help you?" Earthquake Nolan asked.

"You're . . . the sheriff?" Kennedy asked.

"That's right," the sheriff said. "Nolan is my name. And who are you?"

"Lloyd Kennedy."

"Oh," Earthquake said, "you're Kennedy."

"That's right."

The two men stared at each other for a long moment, and for Kennedy it was vaguely disconcerting. He had the distinct impression—and correctly so—that the man didn't like him, and realized that he was alone here with this mountain of a man who, if he came at him, might not even stop after six bullets.

"What do you want?" Earthquake asked.

Kennedy shrugged and said, "I'm just checking in, Sheriff. Want to let you know I'm here."

"You want to rub it in then," Earthquake said.

"That's not it at all, Sheriff," Kennedy said. "We're both after the same thing, aren't we?"

"I'm not sure."

"Well, let me assure you that we are," Kennedy

said. "We both want to get our jobs done, right?"

Earthquake frowned at the man and said frankly, "You're not what I expected."

"You expected a bloodthirsty madman," Kennedy said.

"Something like that."

"Sorry to disappoint you," Kennedy said. "I'm just a man, like any other."

"Maybe . . ."

"I just came by for an exchange of information," Kennedy said, "and to pay my respects."

"What information do you have?"

"Ah, you want me to go first?"

Earthquake's question had been innocent, not contrived, but now he said, "Uh, yeah, okay, I do."

"Well, I have what *you* have, I guess," Kennedy said. "I talked to the people at the bank, and they told me about Will Spenser."

"You talk to Will's ma?"

"Yes, sir, I did," Kennedy said. "A charming lady. I'm sorry she's being put through this."

"You'll be puttin' her through more if you gun down her boy," Earthquake said.

Kennedy laughed disarmingly and said, "Sheriff, I'm not after her boy to gun him down. I'm after the bank robbers. If he's one of them, I hope that he'll give himself up when the time comes."

"And if he don't," Earthquake said, "*then* you'll gun him down."

"As I said, Sheriff," Kennedy said, spreading his hands in a helpless gesture, "I'm only looking to do my job, same as you."

"Well," Earthquake said, obviously not convinced, "I ain't got any more than you. I've combed every inch of this county over the last three days, and I ain't seen hide nor hair of any bank robbers."

"You didn't go *outside* the county?" Kennedy asked.

Earthquake chose to take umbrage at the man's tone of voice.

"I was working alone," he said defensively, "and I had to get back here at the end of every day."

"Sheriff, Sheriff," Kennedy said, "I'm not judging you. I'm sure you're doing everything to the best of your ability."

Earthquake frowned. Kennedy was too smooth, too fast a talker, and he found that he disliked *this* man more than the one he'd *thought* Lloyd Kennedy would be.

"I can't tell you nothin' else."

"What can you tell me," Kennedy asked slyly, "about the boy's father?"

Earthquake frowned. "I don't know who the father is."

"Or whether he's alive or dead?"

"Don't know that neither."

"I see," Kennedy said. "Well, my men and I will be in town tonight, and will probably be pulling out tomorrow morning . . . *if* that's all right with you?"

"Huh? Oh, sure, that's fine with me."

"Well, good," Kennedy said, rubbing his hands together, "very good. Thanks for your, ah, cooperation."

"Yeah," Earthquake said, "sure," although he wasn't so sure he had been all that cooperative.

Outside, Kennedy found Valdez waiting for him, smoking.

"So?" Valdez asked.

"That's a big man," Kennedy said.

"What?"

"Possibly the *biggest* man I've ever seen," Kennedy went on. "Not the tallest, but certainly the biggest."

"What are you talkin' about?" Valdez asked. "What happened in there?"

"Nothing," Kennedy said. When he looked at Valdez his eyes were flat and cold. They were not the eyes that Jean Spenser had seen, or that Sheriff Nolan had seen. "The man doesn't know anything. He won't get in the way."

"And Adams?" Valdez asked.

"Yes," Kennedy said, "it's time that Clint Adams and I met. Where is he?"

"Might be in that cafe," Valdez said. "That's where he was sittin'."

"All right," Kennedy said. "You can take it easy, Soc. Go and join the boys in a drink, or whatever."

"Sure you'll be all right?"

"I'm sure, Soc," Kennedy said, patting the man on the chest, "I'm very sure."

SIXTEEN

Clint looked up and saw Lloyd Kennedy enter the cafe and look around. When the man spotted him, he walked right over to him and fronted the table.

"Clint Adams?"

"That's right."

"Lloyd Kennedy," Kennedy said. "I understand you wanted to talk to me."

Clint sat back and regarded Kennedy. Up close he looked more like forty-five than forty, but that still had to be five or six years off the mark.

"You've got that wrong, Kennedy," Clint said. "It was you who wanted to see me."

Kennedy stared at Clint for a moment, then surprised him with a smile—an engaging, disarming smile. That was when Clint knew that Lloyd Kennedy was everything he had heard he was—and deadly, to boot.

"Maybe we should just talk," Kennedy said. "Mind if I sit?"

"My food is coming," Clint said. "Will you join me for dinner?"

"Well, sure," Kennedy said, sitting. "That's nice of you."

"What will you have?"

"Whatever you're having is fine," Kennedy said magnanimously.

"Steak," Clint said. He waved the waiter over and duplicated his own order. "Bring them out at the same time, will you?"

"Sure, mister," the young waiter said. He frowned, as if he knew something was going on at the table, but couldn't figure out what.

"And bring another coffee cup," Clint said.

"Right away."

He ran for the cup and brought it back, and Clint poured Kennedy a cup.

"Thanks," Kennedy said. "This is real hospitable of you."

"Let's cut the shit, Kennedy," Clint said. "I'm not doing this 'cause I like you. It's just easier than taking you out in the alley and trying to beat the crap out of you."

Kennedy, a tall fit man of fifty-two who routinely whipped men half his age, smiled at Clint, and it was a different kind of smile this time, one that fit more with the man's reputation.

"I'm glad you qualified that by saying 'trying' to beat the crap out of me."

"Oh, I know it wouldn't be easy," Clint said, "but I'd do it."

Kennedy leaned forward, his muscles bunching, and he asked, "What makes you so sure?"

Clint leaned forward and said, "Because my heart is pure, and on the side of right."

Kennedy laughed and sat back, relaxing. "If I thought you really believed that, Adams, I'd be worried about you."

He picked up his cup, sipped the coffee, and put it back down.

"You like surprising people, don't you?" Clint asked.

"Well, when you've got a reputation like mine, people just naturally expect to see me with blood dripping from my mouth," Kennedy said. "But then, you of all people would know all about that, wouldn't you?"

"I know about reputations, yeah," Clint said.

"You see?" Kennedy said. "Do you think people would ever believe that we're just like anybody else? No, because it would ruin their fun."

"You use it to your favor, though," Clint said, "to put people off balance."

Kennedy raised his eyebrows and said, "It works."

"I'm sure it does," Clint said. "Have you talked to the boy's mother yet?"

"Oh, yeah," Kennedy said, "a little while ago. Funny, I didn't fool her. She saw right through me. A smart, good-looking woman."

"I agree."

Kennedy looked directly at Clint, and was about to ask a question when the waiter came with their dinners. They waited while he set the plates down and then retreated.

They both took the time to cut into their meat and taste it, and Kennedy particularly appreciated it. He hadn't even been to his hotel yet, and he was starving.

"What were you going to say?" Clint asked.

Kennedy smiled and sat back again, taking the time to chew what was in his mouth and swallow it.

"I was going to ask what your connection was with the bank robbery."

"None."

"Really?"

"Well, I fired a couple of shots," Clint said, "and maybe even hit one of the robbers, but they all got away."

"I see," Kennedy said. "How did the sheriff do that day?"

"He did his job," Clint said. "Nobody could have asked more from him."

"I doubt that," Kennedy said. "You and I know how town politics works. When this is all over he'll probably get fired. From the size of him, my guess is he'd have to go back to blacksmithing."

Clint hated to admit it, but Kennedy was probably right.

"Did he ask you to join his posse?"

"He did," Clint said. "I chose to mind my own business."

"Good choice," Kennedy said. "And what about the mother?"

"What about her?"

Kennedy cut another chunk of meat, put it in his mouth, and chewed it appreciatively before speaking again.

"Don't tell me *she* didn't come to you for help too," he said then.

"She did."

"And you turned her down too?"

"I did."

"What was the problem?" Kennedy asked, grinning broadly. "Didn't she offer you enough?"

"She *asked* me to help her."

"And you said no," Kennedy said. "You know, I think you're probably a smart man."

"You think so?"

"Oh, yeah," Kennedy said. "Any man who knows when to mind his own business is my idea of a smart man. Tell me, did you turn all of these people down before or after you knew I was being brought in?"

"Before."

Kennedy continued to work on the steak while he talked. Clint's was cooling in the plate. He watched Kennedy eat, and there *was* blood dripping from his mouth.

"And now?"

"Now what?"

"Now, if one of them came back to you for your help, what would you say?" Kennedy asked. "I mean, now that you know I'm here."

Clint's eyes found the crescent-shaped scar alongside Kennedy's left eye. It had been a deep wound, and had healed badly.

"I don't rightly know, Kennedy," Clint said honestly. "I guess I'd just have to wait and see if they *did* come back to me."

Kennedy stopped chewing, and put down his knife and fork.

"Let me give you some advice, Adams," Kennedy said. "*Don't* change your mind."

"Why not?"

"It wouldn't be healthy," Kennedy said. "See, I *know* your rep, and it doesn't impress me."

"That's because you know how unimportant reputations really are," Clint said.

"That's right."

Clint leaned forward and stared Kennedy right in the eyes. "My guess is you also know the real thing when you see it, Lloyd."

"That's right," Kennedy said, standing up, "I do. You know, on one hand I wouldn't want our paths to cross, Adams, because I'd have to kill you. But on the other hand, it might be interesting . . . don't you think?"

"No," Clint said, "I *don't* think, Lloyd. I *think* you're flattering yourself."

Kennedy's eyes were deadly cold, and for a moment he reached up and touched the scar on his face. He rubbed it, as if it was causing him some pain, and then dropped his hand to his side.

"Think it over, Adams," Kennedy said. "My boys and I are goin' out tomorrow." Kennedy stepped back and spread his hands theatrically. "What you do is your business, your decision . . . and you'll have to live with it . . . or die with it."

"That's the way I've always lived my life, Kennedy," Clint said, "and I'm still here."

"There's always a first time," Kennedy said. With that he turned and walked out.

Clint looked down at his steak, and then pushed the plate away so violently that he knocked Kennedy's plate to the floor.

SEVENTEEN

Clint left the cafe and walked over to the sheriff's office. He entered without knocking. Earthquake Nolan was sitting behind the desk, looking miserable. He looked up as Clint entered, and his expression didn't change.

"I understand you had a visit from Lloyd Kennedy," Clint said.

"Yeah, I did," the big man said, frowning. "He wasn't what I expected."

"No," Clint said, "he wasn't what I expected either—he was worse."

Earthquake brightened. "Well, I used to think I was pretty dumb, but I had the same thought too."

"No," Clint said, "you're not dumb."

"Well, thanks, I appreciate that," Earthquake said. "What can I do for you?"

Clint hesitated, then said, "I'd like to know where Mrs. Spenser lives."

Earthquake frowned, as if the question puzzled him, but then he answered it.

"She's got a rooming house down towards the south end of town," he said, actually pointing that way. "Big two-story thing painted a god-awful shade of yellow."

"Thanks."

"Why do you want to talk to her?" Earthquake asked. He actually called out the question, as if trying to get it out before Clint could get through the door.

Clint stopped with his back to the sheriff, then turned and faced him.

"I tell you what, Sheriff," he said. "Let me talk to the lady first, and when I've done that I'll come back and talk to you?"

Suddenly, the man didn't look as miserable or dog-tired as he had before. "Are you gonna help?"

Clint held his hand out to Earthquake, as if showing the man his palm, and said, "Don't go off half cocked. I want to talk to the woman. After I do that, I'll come back. Will you be here?"

"I'll be right here," Earthquake said. "I'll put on a fresh pot of coffee."

"Oh, please," Clint said, "don't," and left.

EIGHTEEN

Clint found the house with no problem, and knocked on the screen door. Some of the windows were lighted, including the downstairs window he assumed was the living room or sitting room window.

The front door opened, and Jeannie Spenser looked out through the screen door. He could tell from the look on her face that she was expecting someone else—maybe Lloyd Kennedy again.

"Mr. Adams?" She sounded puzzled.

"May I talk to you, Mrs. Spenser?" he asked.

"About what?" she asked. "I thought we said what we had to say—"

"I'd like to talk to you about your son and Lloyd Kennedy."

She made a face and said, "That man. He was here today."

"I know."

"In fact, when you knocked I thought—what do you mean, you know?"

"I also talked to him today," he said. "Please, if I could come in and talk to you . . ."

"I'm sorry," she said, and swung the screen door open. "Please, come in."

He entered, and she closed both doors behind them before turning. The house smelled of home cooking.

"My boarders have all had dinner and dessert," she said. "I don't have anything—"

"I've had dinner already, thanks."

"I can offer you some coffee and a piece of pie," she said.

"That'd be fine."

"Please, come into the dining room."

He sat at the dining room table, and she soon returned from the kitchen with a tray bearing a coffee pot, two cups, and two pieces of pie on plates. The pie was apple, and the smell made his mouth water.

She fussed a bit with the coffee and the pie, until he said, "Please, Mrs. Spenser, sit down and let me talk to you."

"I don't know what's wrong with me lately," she said. She sat down, put her hands on the table, then put them in her lap, then folded her arms, and finally put her hands on the table again. "I'm forever fussing," she said, shaking her head.

He put his hand over one of hers and said, "It's understandable. You're worried about your son."

"Worried," she said. "I'm more than worried, I'm *frantic*."

She looked down at his hand, and he removed it and lifted his coffee cup with it.

"May I tell you something?" she asked. "Frankly?"

"Of course."

She hesitated, then let it out in a great rush. "I can't imagine *what* Will could have been doing in that bank with those men."

"Are you admitting that he was there?"

She opened her mouth to speak, and when nothing came out she covered it with her hands. When she finally spoke it was from behind her hands, and with wide, almost shocked eyes.

"People *saw* him," she said. "At least, they *say* they did. Why would they lie?"

"Maybe they're not lying," he said. "Maybe they're just mistaken."

"But . . . but they know him," she said. She took her hands down from her mouth and gestured with them. "He grew up in this town. The people know him. How could they make a mistake like that?"

"Mrs. Spenser," he said, "where is your son now?"

"I don't know," she said, and then she looked at him suspiciously and asked, "Why do you want to know that?"

He put his coffee cup down and looked at her. He hadn't cut into the pie yet, and he wanted to.

"I want to help."

"Why?" she asked, still suspicious. "When I asked you for help you refused me, you turned me down flat. Why do you want to help now?"

"There's nothing . . . there's no hidden motive in my wanting to help," he said. "I don't want Lloyd Kennedy to find your son. It's as simple as that."

"Do you think he would kill Will?" she asked, her voice barely a whisper.

He hesitated, then said, "Yes, I do think that, Mrs. Spenser. I'd like to reach your son before Kennedy does. Can you help me do that?"

"I truly don't know where he is," she said.

"Well, where would he go if he was really in trouble?" Clint asked.

She put her hands down flat on the table and stared at them.

"I know you don't have reason to trust me, Mrs. Spenser," Clint said, "and I know it's hard, but I'm asking you to do just that."

She continued to stare at her hands, and then turned her head to look at him.

"I have to trust someone, I suppose."

He didn't say anything. He didn't want to break her train of thought. If she was working it out for herself, he decided to just let her.

"Mr. Kennedy asked me the same question earlier," she said.

"What did you tell him?"

"I gave him the same answer I gave you," she said, "and then he asked me about Will's father."

"And?"

"I said he was dead."

Clint waited a moment, then said, "But he's not, is he?"

"No," she said, "no, he's not."

"And would Will go to him?"

"Will hasn't seen his father in ten years," she said.

"But he knows where he is?"

"Yes."

"And you think he would go to him?"

"Not under normal circumstances," she said, "but with everything that's happened now, where else *could* he go?"

Clint took Jean Spenser's left hand in his right and asked, "Mrs. Spenser, will you tell me where Will's father lives?"

She thought for a few moments, and then said, "Yes, all right . . ."

NINETEEN

After finally getting Jean Spenser to open up to him, he went back to Sheriff Earthquake Nolan's office, where the sheriff had—against Clint's advice—made a fresh pot of coffee. As Clint entered, Earthquake got up, moved much more quickly than a big man should, and poured two cups of coffee. He carried them back to his desk and sat down, looking up at Clint eagerly.

"Well?"

Clint stared at Earthquake Nolan's open and earnest face and said, "Okay, I'm going to try to help find Will Spenser and keep him alive long enough to try to find out what really happened."

"And help me find the robbers?"

Clint hesitated, not wanting to jump *all* the way in at one time.

"I'm *not* going to do your job for you, Earthquake," he said carefully, "but I don't want Lloyd Kennedy doing it either. If by finding Will Spenser we also find the bank robbers, I'll try to help you bring them in."

"That's great," Earthquake said, almost leaping out of his chair. It was odd to see a man his size acting like an eager child. "When do we start?"

"First of all," Clint said, "you have to be prepared to stay out for more than one whole day. That means someone has to cover here for you, like your first deputy."

Earthquake made a face and said, "I'll talk to him. I just hope nothing goes wrong."

"You can't worry about that, Earthquake," Clint said. "Once we start tracking these men, there's no turning back—unless you want to give it up."

"Look," Earthquake said, "if I knew what to do from the beginning I woulda done it, so I'll do whatever you say, Clint."

"I'll be in charge then?"

"Well," Earthquake said, "I'll be wearing the badge, but you'll be in charge of the, uh, hunt . . . unless you want me to deputize you?"

"No," Clint said, "that won't be necessary."

"Okay, then when do we start?" Earthquake said.

"Early in the morning," Clint said, "at first light. In fact, *before* first light, because Kennedy and *his* men will be moving out at first light. I want to get out there before they do."

"Okay, fine," Earthquake said. "I'll be sleeping right in here, and I'll be ready."

"Okay," Clint said.

"Clint, I really appreciate this," Earthquake said, "even though I know you're not doing it for me."

"It doesn't matter why I'm doing it," Clint said.

"What did you find out from Will Spenser's mother that will help us?" Earthquake asked.

"Will hasn't seen his father in a lot of years," Clint said, "but he knows where he is."

"And now *we* know where he is?"

"That's right," Clint said, "and early tomorrow morning we're going to head out to find him."

When Clint left the office Earthquake was hurrying to find his deputy. He was anxious to bed down in one of the cells. He said he needed to get to bed early if he was going to get up early.

Clint didn't feel the same way. Now that he knew he was going to be going out on a manhunt tomorrow—after days of trying to mind his own business—he was anything but tired. He crossed the street and headed for the saloon. Maybe a few hands of poker, and then he'd go and find the saloon girl called Rose. By then he should be tired enough to get a few hours' sleep, and then he and Earthquake would be on the trail.

God, he was going to have to make sure they had a horse strong enough to carry Earthquake Nolan for as long as this would take.

TWENTY

When Clint entered the saloon, he saw Soc Valdez sitting at a table with two other men. He thought one of the men might be Henny O'Day.

The other two men studied him with interest as he went to the bar, but Valdez made a point of finding his beer very interesting right at that moment.

"Beer?" Ray asked.

"Yeah."

Ray brought the beer, and then inclined his head towards Valdez and the other two.

"They belong to Lloyd Kennedy," Ray said.

"I know."

"You know any of them?"

"One."

"Which one?"

"The one looking inside his beer," Clint said.

"Friend?"

"No."

"What about—"

Clint looked at the man and said, "No more questions, okay, Ray?"

The man took no offense. "Sure, Clint, if you say so," he said, and drifted to the other end of the bar.

Clint held onto his beer and looked around. He decided against poker. His mind just wouldn't be on it. He wondered what Lloyd Kennedy was doing at that moment.

"So that's him, huh?" Henny O'Day said to Valdez.

"That's him," Valdez said without looking up.

"He don't look like much," O'Day said.

"Maybe not," Soc Valdez said, "but that kind of thinkin' got a lot of men killed."

O'Day blew some air out from between his lips, which was supposed to mean that he still wasn't impressed.

Valdez was impressed, but then he had seen Clint Adams in action, and although that had been some years ago, he didn't take comfort from the fact that the man might have lost a step or two. Even two steps slower—or two *seconds*—would still make Clint Adams the fastest man Socrates Valdez had ever seen with a gun.

"He don't look like much," Henny O'Day said again.

Valdez ignored him.

• • •

Tom Connor hated Broken Back, Kansas, but then he hated all the small towns in which he had built his banks. They were making him wealthy, these small towns, but he longed for the day he could forgo them and move into the big cities with his business ventures. He would never be able to do that, though, if people thought that they could get away with *robbing* his banks. It was going to have to be up to Lloyd Kennedy and his bunch to assure people that it couldn't be done, *and* to show the bank robbers themselves the error of their ways.

Lloyd Kennedy looked down at the street from his hotel room window. There was only the one hotel in town, so he knew he was staying at the same place Clint Adams was. He had no idea what room Clint was in, though he knew he could find out if he wanted to. At the moment, there was no reason to do so.

Kennedy looked at the whore in his bed. She was lying with her back to him, her big ass bare. He felt nothing looking at her, and he had felt nothing emotionally while he had been in bed with her. All he had felt was the physical release that he'd needed. He was keeping her around now because he knew he'd need it again during the night, probably more than once. He was starting a hunt tomorrow, and on a hunt he never thought about sex, so he always got his fill the night before.

He knew three of his men were in the saloon, Valdez among them. He often wondered if Soc Valdez even liked women, but then what the man liked or disliked was up to him. Valdez had been with Kennedy a long time, and as long as the man did his job Kennedy didn't care if he fucked warthogs.

His other two men, he knew, were at the local whorehouse. Kennedy preferred to get a woman and bring her up to his own room where he could have her whenever he wanted her. Also, he hated hearing the sounds around him of other people's so-called pleasures.

He reached for a cigar on the table near the window and lit it, unmindful that the glow from the match might reveal to anyone standing outside that he was completely naked. He doused the match, inhaled deeply, and let the smoke out in a steady, almost solid-looking stream.

Clint Adams was a potential problem. There was no way around that. Kennedy admitted that he had probably been foolish, bracing Adams the way he had. It had almost been a challenge, one that he had not—at that particular moment—been able to resist. Imagine going up against the Gunsmith and coming out on top.

Lloyd Kennedy had done just about everything *else* in his life he'd ever wanted to, so why not this?

The thought of besting a man like Clint Adams excited him, and his penis began to inflate. He left the window, walked over to the bed, and woke the whore with a resounding slap on her wide ass.

TWENTY-ONE

Clint awoke the next morning with Rose down between his legs. Her avid mouth was bringing him to the brink of explosion, and he had to reach down and stop her so that, now that he was awake, he could fully enjoy her charms before getting dressed and leaving town for who knows how long.

Returning to his hotel last night with Rose, Clint had been surprised to find Sherry Lance barring his path.

"You go on ahead, Rose," he'd said. "I'll catch up with you."

Rose had walked past Sherry, the two women coolly sizing one another up.

"What can I do for you, Sherry?" he'd asked.

"I understand you're going after the bank robbers with the sheriff."

He didn't ask her how she had found out.

"That's right."

"Clint," she said, softening her tone, "I've been very foolish. I . . . no man has ever made me feel the way you did when we were together. Please, before you leave, I—I'd like to try and make it up to you."

"Well, Sherry," Clint said, "as you can see I have a previous engagement."

"With *her*?" Sherry asked, growing angry. "That saloon . . . *tart*?"

"At least that saloon tart is honest about her feelings," Clint said. "You wanted to be with me until you realized that your money wasn't as important to me as it was to you."

"Clint," she said, her tone becoming seductive, "I told you I was foolish, but I want to make it up to you."

"I'm sorry, Sherry," he said. "You were wonderful in bed. It's too bad you were a different person when we *weren't* in bed."

"Why, you can't—"

"Excuse me," he had said, and walked by her to join Rose at the hotel.

Now Rose was enthusiastically trying to change Clint's mind about leaving town. She was sitting astride him, with his rigid penis buried inside her. Her hands were busy, and her mouth was roaming over his neck and chest, teasing his nipples . . .

"You don't really want to leave town, do

you?" she said. "You don't really want to leave Rose . . ."

"Actually, Rose," he said, "I don't, but I don't have much choice at this point."

She sat back on him then and looked down at him with a sad look on her face.

"When will you be back?" she asked.

"When the job's done, I guess."

"Well," she said, sliding her hands down over his belly, "I'll be here waiting."

When Clint reached the sheriff's office he went inside without knocking. He had fully expected to have to wake Earthquake Nolan, but the man was up—just barely. He was seated behind his desk with a cup of coffee in both hands, and his eyes were barely open.

"Ready?" Clint asked.

"I'm ready," Earthquake said.

"What about the horses?" Clint asked.

"I have the key to the livery stable," the sheriff said. "What about supplies?"

"We'll travel light," Clint said, "and pick up what we need along the way."

Earthquake stared at him and asked, "What about food?"

"We'll make do along the way," Clint said. "Don't worry, we'll have water."

"Oh, fine," Earthquake said, standing up. "Oh, well, at least I'll be able to make coffee."

"Oh, no," Clint said, "I'll be making the coffee, Sheriff. We agree on that right now, or I'm not going."

Earthquake looked puzzled, and stared down at his half-full coffee cup. "Is my coffee that bad?"

"It's worse than bad," Clint said. "It's vile."

Earthquake looked hurt now, but he said, "Well, all right then. If you feel that strongly about it, you can make the coffee."

"Good," Clint said. "Then we're ready to move out."

"We're ready, I guess," Earthquake said. He grabbed his hat and picked up a rifle.

"No gunbelt?" Clint asked.

Looking sheepish, Earthquake Nolan said, "The buckle broke. That's always happening. I can never find one that fits me."

The sheriff opened a drawer, took out his handgun, and tucked it into his belt.

"That'll have to be good enough then," Clint said. "Let's go."

As Clint Adams and Sheriff Earthquake Nolan left the lawman's office, a man standing in the shadows across the street watched them. Soc Valdez had to admit that Lloyd Kennedy was right, again. Adams and Nolan were leaving even *before* first light, hoping to get the jump on Kennedy and his men.

Well, Valdez also had to admit that he had never known *anyone* to get the jump on Lloyd Kennedy, and that *included* Clint Adams, the Gunsmith.

TWENTY-TWO

Jeannie Spenser had told Clint that Will Spenser's father—her husband, since they had never divorced—was living in a town called Dayville, about three days' ride from Broken Back but still in Kansas.

"His name's Victor Spenser," Clint told Earthquake.

"And they're still married, even though he left so long ago?" the sheriff asked.

"Mrs. Spenser says that she took her marriage vows very seriously," Clint said.

"She's a loyal woman," Earthquake said.

Clint felt she was a foolish woman. She was an attractive woman, and could have found herself another man and started a new life. She *still* could, but that wasn't his business. His only involvement with her right now was in trying to keep her son alive.

Earthquake was interested in that, and finally asked the question after several hours on the trail. "Why are you doing this?"

"I thought we went through that," Clint answered.

"No," Earthquake said, "I mean *really*, why'd you change your mind after turning me down, *and* turning down Mrs. Spenser when she practically *begged* you for your help?"

Clint took a few moments to form his reply before he started speaking. "I don't know."

"What?"

"I've spent a lot of time during my life minding other people's business," Clint said. "Usually it's because I'm asked and I can't say no."

"So this time you just wanted to say no?"

"I was *determined* to say no and stay out of it," Clint said.

"So what changed your mind?"

"Lloyd Kennedy," Clint said simply. "I just don't like the man's methods, and if there's even the slightest chance that Will Spenser is innocent—or even if there were some, uh, special circumstances—I'd like the boy to have a fair chance to explain."

Earthquake stared at him and said, "*That's* why?"

"That's why," Clint said. "What did you think it was?"

"I don't know . . . I, uh, thought maybe you were, uh, interested in his mother . . ."

"No," Clint said, "that's not the case."

"So . . . you just want to keep the boy alive?" Earthquake asked. He seemed to be having a problem with that as the only answer.

"That's right," Clint said. "Or maybe I just want to make sure Lloyd Kennedy fails this time."

"Oh," Earthquake said, "oh, well, I can understand *that*."

That answer seemed much more like what Earthquake was expecting to hear. In fact, it seemed to satisfy him so much that he fell silent and stayed that way until they made camp for the night.

Clint allowed Earthquake to build the fire, but they stuck to their deal and Clint was the one who made the pot of coffee.

"It's a little weak, isn't it?" Earthquake asked after taking a sip. He was staring down into the cup, as if the contents offended him.

Traditionally, trail coffee was the strongest coffee there was, and Clint prided himself on liking his coffee *very* black and *very* strong. This pot was exactly to his liking.

"*I* don't think so," he said defensively, holding a cup of his own.

Earthquake swirled the liquid in his cup, tasted it again, then shrugged.

"Tell me something," Clint said.

"What?"

"Where'd the name Earthquake come from?"

The big man looked at him, looked down at

himself, and then said, "Are you serious?"

"No—I mean, I know you're big—"

"My mother used to say that when I walked the ground moved," he said. "My pa said it was like an earthquake, so that's what everybody called me from that time on."

"How old were you then?"

"I don't know," he said with a shrug of his massive shoulders. "Two, three?"

Clint didn't say anything, but how could parents call a two- or three-year-old boy "Earthquake"? It sounded cruel to him.

"What's your real name?"

"Ha," Earthquake laughed, shaking his head and wagging a thick forefinger at Clint. "I'll never tell you that."

"Is it that bad?"

"It's worse," Earthquake said. "On my deathbed maybe I'll tell someone, but not now."

"How bad could it be?" Clint asked.

Earthquake looked at Clint and said, "No."

They dined on hardtack. When they got to Dayville, maybe they'd pick up some bacon. Clint didn't want to carry any more than that.

He sat across the fire from Earthquake and studied his new traveling partner. Everything about the man seemed to be round—his shoulders, his back, his big belly. He was not muscular by any means, but Clint still had the feeling that he had not ever met a stronger man.

"We'll sit watches," Clint said.

"Why?" Earthquake asked. "Aren't we the hunters, not the hunted?"

"Right now we are," Clint said, "but it's been my experience that those roles can be very quickly reversed. Just to play it on the safe side, I'll take the first watch and wake you in three hours."

"Three hours each?" Earthquake asked, looking dubious. "That doesn't allow for much sleep."

"I want to get an early start again," Clint said. "Maybe we can make good time to Dayville."

"Do you think the boy will be there?"

"I don't know, Earthquake," Clint said. "It's just a place to start, which is what every manhunt begins with."

"I guess so," Earthquake said. He rolled himself up in his blanket and then looked up at Clint. "Somehow, when I took this job I didn't think it would ever come to this. I thought I'd be keeping drunks in line, shooting stray dogs, and such."

"It's all part of the same job, Earthquake," Clint said. "You've got to be prepared to do it all."

"Yeah," Earthquake said, and lay down.

Clint figured the man was having second thoughts about his career plans. Personally, after having watched the man in action, he thought it was probably a good idea.

TWENTY-THREE

Socrates Valdez had spent many nights without the benefit of a fire, as he was spending this one. From his vantage point he could see Clint Adams and Earthquake Nolan's camp very clearly. They were drinking coffee, and as much as he would have liked a cup, he was able to watch dispassionately. This was one of Valdez's talents: trailing and watching without ever being seen himself, and controlling his wants and needs by virtue of his willpower. Many was the time he'd had to stay for days in one place without benefit of food or water, or even the opportunity to relieve himself. This, then—watching the two men drink coffee—was a minor annoyance and nothing more.

He sat comfortably on the ground while he saw the big man roll himself up in a blanket and Clint Adams settle down to stand watch. Adams was a careful man, there was no denying that. Valdez made a mental note to be even *more* careful the next day while following them.

A half a day behind Socrates Valdez, Henny O'Day and the other men camped around a fire and shared bacon, beans, biscuits, and coffee. After dinner O'Day produced a bottle of whiskey and offered it around.

"Put that away," Kennedy said.

O'Day looked at Kennedy. The others watched. They had seen Henny O'Day try to stand up to Lloyd Kennedy many times, and it never failed to fascinate them. No matter how many times Kennedy stared O'Day down, the man insisted on trying again at some point.

"It's just a bottle of whiskey, Boss," O'Day said. "A couple of sips."

"Put the damn jug away, Henny," Kennedy said coldly.

"Boss—"

Kennedy silenced O'Day by pointing his finger at him.

"Don't try me tonight, Henny," Kennedy said. "I'm in no mood."

O'Day hesitated a moment, then said, "Okay, okay," and put the bottle away.

They had spent the day following the trail left by Soc Valdez as *he* followed Adams and the sheriff. Kennedy laughed at the idea that Clint Adams thought he could get the jump on him. True, Adams had had some experience hunting men, but compared with Lloyd Kennedy the man was a rank amateur, as Kennedy's plan plainly showed.

Clint Adams would lead Soc Valdez to the Spenser woman's husband, and Valdez in turn would mark the way for Kennedy and the others to follow. It was such a simple plan that there was no way it could *fail* to work.

So Kennedy wondered why he was feeling uneasy about it.

TWENTY-FOUR

"What's wrong?" Earthquake asked.

They were ten miles from the town of Dayville, and Clint suddenly reined Duke in. He didn't turn around or anything, he just stopped and sat there. It looked like he was listening to something.

"What is it?" Earthquake asked again. "What do you hear?"

"I don't know," Clint said, then quickly added, "Don't look around, don't *turn* around."

Earthquake froze—which in a way was even *more* of a giveaway—and asked, "What's going on?"

"Something just occurred to me."

"What?"

"Don't sit so stiffly, Earthquake," Clint said. "Relax in the saddle."

Earthquake made an effort, and it was *marginally* better than before. He still looked like he was waiting for a blow from behind.

"I just realized that we could have someone trailing us," Clint said.

"Have you seen anybody?"

"No."

"Well . . . wouldn't you? I mean, you've *done* this before."

"I would with most people."

"What does *that* mean?"

"It means," Clint said, "that if Soc Valdez is back there following us, I *wouldn't* see him."

"Why not?"

"Because this is his specialty," Clint said. "If he makes a mistake I'd see him, but if he doesn't make a mistake there's no way I would know he was there."

"So, in other words, we don't *know* that we're being tailed?"

"Right."

"But we *might* be?"

"Right again."

"Well, then," Earthquake said very slowly, "how do we find out?"

"Good question," Clint said, rubbing his jaw, "very good question. Come on, let's ride slow while I think about it."

As they rode along Earthquake was hard put *not* to turn around and look behind them.

"How about I double back and come up behind him?" the big man asked.

"Behind who?"

"Well . . . whoever is following us."

"There might not be *anyone* following us, Earthquake," Clint said. "And if there was, you wouldn't be able to come up from behind him."

"*You* would?"

Clint hesitated and then said, "Ah, I don't know. If it's who I think it is, I don't *know* if I could sneak up behind him."

"He's good, this fella who *might* be following us?" Earthquake asked.

"Yes," Clint said, "he's good . . . this fella who *might* be following us."

"So what do we do?"

Clint looked at Earthquake and said, "*We* are going to keep quiet so I can think."

"Okay, okay," Earthquake said, shaking his head. "I'm just askin' . . . "

"Okay . . ."

"No harm in askin', is there?"

"Earthquake!"

"All right . . . I just don't like the idea that I'm bein' followed . . . "

"Just sit on your tongue for a couple of minutes, okay?" Clint asked.

He fell silent then and Clint had time to think, but it didn't help much. There wasn't much to consider. There were only two options. Either they were being followed, in which case they couldn't afford to lead their tail to Will Spenser's father, or they *weren't* being followed, in which case they could just ride into Dayville without fear of exposing anyone to danger.

If they were being followed there was no doubt who it was. Kennedy would have been smart enough to send Valdez, because the Mexican was good at this.

"Made up your mind yet?" Earthquake asked.

Clint gave him a quick look which silenced him for a few more minutes.

What they could have done was ride right past Dayville, and try to lead their tail someplace where they could lose him, but that would have taken time. Riding into Dayville with Soc Valdez on their tail wouldn't actually give anything away. It was when it looked like they were going to *stay* in Dayville that Valdez would become most interested. So they had to make it look like they *weren't* staying in Dayville, that the town of Dayville was *not* their intended goal . . .

"Now—"

"Yes," Clint said, cutting him off, "I have an idea . . . now!"

TWENTY-FIVE

The rode into Dayville toward evening of the third day. They'd made good time. Clint felt that time was important, because so much of it had been wasted since the bank was hit. Anything could have happened by now. The money could have been split, the robbers could have gone their own ways . . . Canada . . . Mexico . . . who knows? Will Spenser could have been dead for all Clint knew. So time was important. That was why he hadn't wanted to bother with bypassing Dayville.

"Where does the father live?" Earthquake asked, looking around.

"Don't do that," Clint said.

"What?"

"Don't look like you're looking for somebody," Clint said. "We're supposed to be stopping for supplies, remember?"

"Oh, okay," Earthquake said, "only there's somethin' you should know about me."

"What?"

"I ain't any better an actor than I am a sheriff," the big man said.

"Don't worry, Earthquake," Clint said. "I'll do all the talking."

"Good," Earthquake said.

They dismounted and tied their horses in front of the general store, as if they really were stopping to pick up supplies. Earthquake stopped for a moment to look Duke over. He'd admired the big black gelding from the first time he'd seen him.

"You know," he said then, "I should be riding Duke. He's big enough to carry me."

"Big enough to throw you too," Clint said. "Come on, let's go inside."

Earthquake followed Clint up onto the boardwalk and into the general store. There were a couple of women inside who stopped and gaped at the size of the big lawman. He just smiled at them and tipped his hat, and they hurried outside.

Clint walked up to the counter where a white-haired man stood wearing an apron.

"Can I help you?"

"I hope you can," Clint said. "I'm looking for a man named Victor Spenser. Do you know him?"

"Victor?" the man said. "Sure, I know him."

"Can you tell me where I can find him?"

"Sure," the man said. "Over to the undertaker's."

Earthquake moved closer to the counter and looked at the man—actually, he loomed over him, and the man even took a step back.

"He's the undertaker?" the lawman asked.

"No," the man said, "he's at the undertaker's."

"Oh," Earthquake said, "he's making arrangements for somebody."

"You could say that," the man said.

"Wait a minute," Clint said. "Never mind what *we* could say. What are *you* trying to say?"

"I'm tryin' to tell you that Victor Spenser is over to the undertaker's office."

Clint waited a beat and then asked, "And *why* is he over to the undertaker's?"

"Because," the man said, speaking slowly, "he's dead."

"What?" Earthquake said.

Clint stared at the storekeeper, thought about asking him what had happened, then decided that there were better people to ask about that.

"Okay," he said finally, "thank you."

"B-but wha—" Earthquake started, but Clint grabbed his arm to silence him.

"Let's go outside," he said.

They stepped outside and Clint looked up and down the street.

"Well, one thing this does for us," he said.

"What?"

He looked at Earthquake and said, "We don't have to worry about being followed here anymore."

TWENTY-SIX

They stopped at the undertaker's first, to make sure they were talking about the same Victor Spenser.

"I don't know what I can tell you," the undertaker said. "He's the only Victor Spenser I've got here. How am I supposed to know if he's *your* Victor Spenser?"

Clint stared down at the man who was spread out on the table. He'd been shot just the day before, according to the undertaker. Clint took a good look at the face. He didn't know what Will Spenser looked like, so he couldn't tell if there was a resemblance. The dead man did have blond hair, though, and he was about the right age.

"I can't tell you anything about the incident," the undertaker said.

"I'm not asking you about it," Clint said. "I'll talk to the sheriff about that."

"What about the burial?" the undertaker asked.

Clint was already on his way out, and he turned to answer.

"What would you have done if I hadn't come in asking about him?" Clint asked.

"Hell," the undertaker said, "I'd have paid for it out of his belongings."

"Then do it," Clint said, and left.

Earthquake was waiting outside. He hadn't wanted to go inside to look at the dead man. There was no need, he'd said, since he'd never met the man and wouldn't have been able to identify him anyway.

Clint just thought that the big man didn't like looking at dead people. He couldn't blame him for that, but it was only another indication that Earthquake Nolan should find another line of work.

"Was it him?"

"How do I know?" Clint said. "It could be him, but there's no way to be sure. According to the undertaker he's the only Victor Spenser in town. So, yeah, I guess that means it's him."

"Damn!" Earthquake said. "Now what do we do?"

Clint looked at Earthquake and saw that the man had taken off his badge.

"Put your tin star back on and we'll go and talk to the local sheriff."

• • •

The sheriff's name was Cal Bennett, and he was taken aback for a moment by the size of his colleague from Broken Back.

"What happened to Sheriff Holcomb?" he asked.

"He ain't sheriff no more," Earthquake said.

It occurred to Clint then that Earthquake Nolan could be a very menacing figure to anyone who didn't know him. That was something that might come in handy.

"I see," Bennett said. He was a small, bandy-legged man in his fifties with a gray mustache. His *lack* of size only increased the effect of Earthquake's.

The sheriff looked at Clint and asked, "Is this your deputy?"

"No," Earthquake said, "Mr. Clint Adams here is just, uh, assisting me."

Clint had told Earthquake to *act* like a sheriff when they were with the local law.

"I see," Bennett said again. "Well, what can I do for you, Sheriff?"

"Well, we, uh, Mr. Adams and I, that is, came to town to talk to one of your citizens."

"Oh? Which one might that be?"

"Victor Spenser?"

"Oh," Bennett said, "oh, well, I guess that means you're out of luck."

"So we heard," Clint said. "We've already talked to the undertaker."

"So . . . I guess you wanna know what happened, huh?" Bennett asked.

Clint looked at Earthquake, who said, "Oh, yeah, we wanna know what happened . . . we sure do . . ."

"Well," Bennett said, "I can't rightly say I know."

"How's that?" Clint asked.

"Well, we all heard some shots coming from Spenser's store—he, uh, ran the hardware store. I don't know if you knew that."

"We didn't," Clint said. "Go on."

"Well . . . like I said, we heard shots and a bunch of us ran down there. He was lying behind his counter, already dead. Shot to pieces, actually."

"Who did it?" Earthquake asked.

"Damned if I know."

"What are you doing to find out?" Clint asked.

"Not much," Bennett said. "I ain't no detective. Somebody shot him and ran off. Nothing was even stolen. What am I supposed to do?"

"How about tracking them?"

"I ain't a tracker either, mister," Bennett said. "I know what I can do, and what I can't do, and I don't get 'em mixed up."

Clint was tempted to say something he might regret, and decided against it.

"Did you ask any questions around town?" Clint asked. "Try to find some witnesses?"

"Sure I did, but nobody saw nothin'," Bennett said.

"Would you mind if we asked around some?" Clint asked.

"Yeah," Earthquake said, "would you mind?"

When he answered, Sheriff Bennett was looking at Earthquake, and not Clint.

"Sure," he said, "why would I mind?"

TWENTY-SEVEN

Soc Valdez didn't like it.

He didn't like it because he couldn't figure it out. Figuring things out was not Socrates Valdez's strong suit. He wasn't smart enough, and he knew it. That was what made him and Lloyd Kennedy such a good team. Of course, Soc Valdez was the only one of the two who thought of them as a team.

Anyway, he was watching Clint Adams and Earthquake Nolan from a vantage point on a ridge above Dayville. They were easy to spot, thanks to the size of the sheriff from Broken Back.

First they went to the general store, then the undertaker's, and then the sheriff's office.

What did all of that mean?

And where were they going next?

He wished Kennedy was there.

Lloyd Kennedy was pushing. Instead of half a day behind Soc Valdez, they were now only a few hours. He hoped to catch up to him before nightfall. Valdez had followed Adams long enough alone. It was time for Kennedy to get involved in the action. If Adams hadn't led them to the kid's old man by now, it was because he *knew* he was being followed.

It was time to make the next move.

TWENTY-EIGHT

"What do we do now?" Earthquake asked. "Go back to Broken Back?"

"Earthquake," Clint said, shaking his head, "you never catch anybody you're hunting for by going back home. You just keep going until you *do* catch them."

The big man frowned and asked, "But . . . what if you *never* catch them?"

Clint stared at him, then just shook his head and put his hand on the man's massive right shoulder. "You go to the hotel and check us in, okay? One room each."

"Okay. What are you gonna do?"

"I'm going to take care of the horses, and then walk around a bit and ask some questions."

"Should I ask some questions?"

"No," Clint said quickly, "no, you'll just scare

people. Why don't you get yourself something to eat?"

"What about you?"

"I'll eat later," Clint said. "It's okay, you can go eat."

Earthquake's eyes lit up and he said, "All right."

Clint patted him on the shoulder and said, "I'll meet you . . . over there—" he pointed to the saloon across the street "—in two hours. All right? Two hours."

"Two hours?" Earthquake repeated, looking disappointed. "I thought you said I'd have time to eat!"

Clint took Duke and Earthquake's bay over to the livery and had them taken care of. After that he walked over to Spenser's hardware store, which was closed and locked. The stores around it were open and doing business, however, and he went into each of them in turn and asked his questions. After that he went across the street and asked the same questions.

In one store—right next to Spenser's—he asked where Spenser had lived. As it turned out, Spenser had had a house at the south end of town, just about where Jeannie Spenser had her boardinghouse in Broken Back.

Spenser had had neighbors also, and Clint even talked to them. By the time he went to meet Earthquake, he had a pretty good picture of what had taken place.

TWENTY-NINE

As darkness started to fall on Dayville, Lloyd Kennedy and the rest of his men caught up to Soc Valdez, who heard them coming. He was on his feet waiting when they reached him.

"See? I told you he'd hear us comin'," Henny O'Day said to the others with a big smile. "God-damned Mexican's got ears like a cat."

"Better than a cat," Kennedy said. He dismounted, handed his horse over to one of the other men, and then fronted Valdez.

"Come over here," Valdez said. "You can see the town from here."

Kennedy followed him, and found himself looking down at Dayville with a clear view. Once it was dark, though, there wouldn't be much to see.

"Good spot," he said. "What have you seen?"

Valdez told Kennedy what had been going on, and he watched as the man's face tightened.

"You know what it means, right?" Soc Valdez asked Kennedy.

"If they came here looking for the kid's father," Kennedy said, "it doesn't sound good. Why would they go to the undertaker's, and then to the sheriff?"

It suddenly dawned on Valdez and he said, "Because he's dead?"

"Right."

"And if the father is dead, there's no trail," Valdez went on.

Kennedy smiled at the Mexican and said, "Don't get carried away with your brain power, Soc. That *isn't* necessarily true."

"Why not?"

"Because there's still the question of *how* he was killed, isn't there?"

"How do we find out?"

"Well," Kennedy said, "I guess one of us is just going to have to go down there and find out."

"Which one?" Valdez asked. Adams knew him and Kennedy, and might even remember the others.

"I don't know," Kennedy said. "Let's make camp and I'll think about it a little more."

THIRTY

When Clint entered the saloon, Earthquake Nolan was nowhere to be seen. Clint remembered that the man didn't seem to think that two hours would be long enough for him to eat. He was probably still sitting somewhere working on his dinner.

Clint went to the bar and found a spot to elbow into. The saloon was doing a brisk business, as was usually the case in any town when it started to get dark. Even though the place was crowded, Earthquake certainly would have stuck out of the crowd if he was there.

It took Clint a few moments to get the bartender's attention, and then he ordered a beer. The man brought it, but Clint didn't have a chance to engage the man in any small talk. It was one of the few times he had ever seen a bartender too busy to talk.

He was nursing the beer when he heard Spenser's name from someone further down the bar. He eavesdropped on the conversation that was taking place.

" . . . something when one of our best citizens, Vic Spenser, gets killed and the sheriff doesn't do a thing about it."

"What's he supposed to do?" someone else asked. "You know he ain't gonna go out and hunt the killers down—even if he knew who they were."

"All he would have had to do was ask around," the first man said. "He'd be sure to find somebody who saw something, but he never bothered to ask."

It was as Clint had thought. The sheriff hadn't even tried to find out who had killed Spenser. Clint had found out, though. He'd found out a few things, just by asking around.

At that moment something happened, something that drew everyone's attention to the front doors. Clint turned and saw what it was.

Earthquake.

The big lawman was standing just inside the batwing doors, looking around for Clint. When he saw him he grinned and started towards the bar.

It was comical. Men moved out of his way so they wouldn't be trampled, and when he reached the bar several men moved away, creating an opening big enough for him to belly up to the bar.

"Want a beer?" Clint asked.

"Sure."

There was some food stuck in Earthquake's beard, enough to tell Clint that the man had had chicken for dinner, greasy chicken.

"Get the bartender's attention," Clint said to Earthquake. He was curious to see how long it would take the bartender to notice him.

"Bartender!" Earthquake bellowed, and the bartender hurried down the bar.

"What can I get you?"

"A beer."

"Comin' up."

Clint had never seen a bartender fetch a beer so quickly before.

"Anything else?"

"No," Earthquake said. "That's all."

Clint was fascinated by the effect Earthquake had on the men in the saloon. Because of his size and countenance, men tried to stare at him without *seeming* to stare at him, tried to stay out of his way, but were drawn to him. And Clint could see by the looks on most of their faces that they were frightened of him.

"Come on, Earthquake," Clint said. "Let's go and sit down. We have a lot to talk about."

"You found out something?"

"I found out a lot," Clint said. "Why don't you go and find us a table."

"Sure."

Clint turned to the bartender, and benefited from the fact that he was now with Earthquake. The man rushed over to see what he wanted.

"What can I get you?"

"Can I get something to eat here?"

"I can probably rustle you up some kind of sandwich," the bartender said. "Would that be good enough?"

"Sure," Clint said. "That'd be fine."

"I'll, uh, bring it over to you."

"Fine."

Clint turned in time to see three men get up from a table to let Earthquake sit down.

"Bring it over to that table," he told the bartender, and started across the room.

THIRTY-ONE

Clint sat down across from Earthquake, who had sat with his back to the room. If the man had any intention of pursuing his career in law enforcement, Clint would have to lecture him about that. He was blissfully ignorant of the target his wide back made.

"So what'd you find out?" Earthquake asked.

"Wait a minute," Clint said. He flagged a saloon girl who was going by.

"Can I help you?" she asked, putting her hands on her hips and wagging them saucily back and forth.

"The bartender is going to bring me a sandwich of some kind," he said. "Would you have him bring a big napkin as well?"

"Sure," she said. "In fact, I'll bring it all over here myself."

She had short red hair, almost as short as a boy's, and she was as slim as a boy too. Her skin, though, was smooth and creamy, by far her best feature, and she wore a dress that showed most of it off. She also had a wonderful pair of legs.

"Thanks," he said, and she went off, her hips twitching.

"Why do you need a napkin if all you're eatin' is a sandwich?" Earthquake asked. His face said that this was something he was really puzzling over.

"The napkin is not for me, Earthquake," Clint said. "It's for you."

"For me?" Earthquake said, puzzled.

"You still got half your dinner in your beard, Earthquake."

"Huh," the big man said, touching his beard and coming away with a small chunk of chicken. He examined it, and then ate it. Clint reminded himself never to eat in a restaurant with the man. "Just crumbs," Earthquake said.

"And grease," Clint added.

"Okay, so when the napkin comes I'll clean up," Earthquake said. "Tell me what you found out."

"Well, first off, some of Spenser's neighbors saw a visitor here a couple of days ago. He was about eighteen or so, and the description fits Will Spenser."

"Then he found his father."

"It looks that way," Clint said. "Only thing is, people say that the two didn't look happy with each other. They argued a lot for a couple of days, and then the kid left town."

Earthquake frowned. "That don't help us at all," he said.

"Yes, it does."

"How?"

"I found a witness to the killing," Clint said.

"What? Who?"

"It was a man who'd been going into Spenser's hardware store to buy something. When he got to the door Spenser was inside arguing with some men."

"Did you get a description of the men?"

"The witness couldn't quite see them. There were two of them, though," Clint added.

"And they killed him?"

"The witness hid outside," Clint said. "He says that the men were asking Spenser where the kid was, and where some money was. When Spenser kept telling them he didn't know anything about the kid or the money, they started hitting him. According to the witness, Spenser must have tried for a gun and the two men shot him."

"What happened then?"

"The witness ran off."

"How come he hasn't told this to the sheriff?" Earthquake asked.

"He says the sheriff hasn't asked him."

"Huh," Earthquake said, "and I thought *I* was a bad lawman."

The saloon girl came over with Clint's sandwich, which unfortunately looked like chicken.

It reminded him of the chicken in Earthquake's beard.

"Here's the napkin," she said to Clint, handing it to him. It was checkerboard red and white.

"Thanks."

"Anything else?"

"Not right now."

"You be sure to tell me when, hear?"

"I hear."

As she walked away Earthquake watched her go, then said to Clint, "Women like you, huh?"

"Here," Clint said, tossing the man the napkin. "Clean your face."

Clint drank his beer while Earthquake wiped his face with the napkin. A couple of stray pieces of chicken fell from his face into his lap.

"Howzat?" the big man asked, putting the napkin down.

"You're beautiful."

Earthquake looked down at Clint's sandwich and asked, "Ain't you gonna eat that?"

Clint looked at the sandwich. He *would* have eaten it if it had been anything but chicken.

"No," he said, "it's all yours."

THIRTY-TWO

Earthquake Nolan made short work of the chicken sandwich—to the absolute fascination of others at nearby tables—and then he and Clint ordered two more beers from the red-haired saloon girl, which she was only too happy to bring over.

"My name's Mitzi," she said when she brought the beers. She was talking directly to Clint. "Don't forget me, all right?"

Earthquake watched her walk away again, and then said again, "Women like you, huh?"

"I don't have food in my beard," Clint said, rolling his eyes.

Earthquake frowned, squinted, and said, "You don't *have* a beard."

"Nice of you to notice."

Earthquake ignored the comment—or didn't hear it—looked around a bit, and then asked,

"Well, what do we do now?"

"Well, this is the way it sounds to me," Clint said. "It sounds like Will Spenser *was* in the robbery, and that soon after they left Broken Back he must have taken off with the money."

"Holy . . ." Earthquake said, his eyes bugging out. "That kid? He stole from his own partners? Mrs. Spenser ain't gonna be happy to hear that."

"She'll have to deal with it," Clint said. "That is, if we can find her son alive."

"Kennedy, you mean?"

"I mean Lloyd Kennedy and his men *and* the bank robbers," Clint said. "They're looking for him too. I mean, they killed his father when he wouldn't tell them where he was."

"Do you think his old man knew?"

"I don't think so," Clint said, warming to his subject. He thought he had it pretty much figured out. "I think the kid found his old man, told him what he'd done, and the old man didn't agree with him. I think *that's* what people saw them fighting about."

"Makes sense to me," Earthquake said. "So what do we do now?"

"We've got to find that kid," Clint said. "If we find him first, we'll find the money too."

"Okay, let's do it," Earthquake said eagerly. Then he leaned his elbows on the table and asked, "Uh, *how* do we do it?"

Clint shook his head and said, "I haven't the faintest idea."

THIRTY-THREE

When the man entered the saloon Clint couldn't believe it. Did Kennedy really think he could send one of his men into town without Clint recognizing him? Maybe . . . maybe he *did* think that. Maybe he figured Clint didn't have time to see all of the men in Broken Back. But that was maybe. Lloyd Kennedy didn't strike Clint as the kind of man who put stock in *maybe*.

"What's wrong?" Earthquake asked.

"One of Lloyd Kennedy's men just walked in."

Earthquake froze. "Should I not turn around?"

"No, it's okay," Clint said. "You can look. I think we're *supposed* to see him."

Earthquake turned, looked around, then looked at Clint and said, "Where? Which one?"

"Over by the bar, second . . . no, third from the left. He's getting a beer now from the bartender."

Earthquake turned again to look.

"See him?"

"I see him," Earthquake said. He looked at Clint again and asked, "What do we do?"

"Nothing," Clint said.

"Why nothing?"

"Because the only reason Kennedy would send him in is to force us to do something."

"Like what?"

"Like question him."

"About what?"

Clint hoped that the man's bulk would come in *very* handy in the near future, because his brain was just going to waste.

"About anything," Clint said. "He just wants us kept busy."

"Why?" Earthquake asked. "What's Kennedy gonna be doing?"

"I don't know," Clint said, pushing his chair back, "but let's find out."

Clint knew it was hopeless to try to leave with Earthquake and go completely unnoticed, but maybe they could just move out of the saloon quietly, without arousing *everyone's* attention.

Earthquake pushed his chair back so quickly to keep up with Clint that one of the legs protested and broke with a loud crack. He went tumbling over backward, rolled into a table of four, and took everyone and everything to the floor with him.

Well, so much for leaving quietly.

• • •

"What did you find out?" Kennedy asked Henny O'Day.

"There was a Spenser living here, but he's dead," O'Day said. "I got that from the undertaker. He, uh, wasn't in a hurry to talk, but I convinced him."

Kennedy gave the man a hard look and said, "You didn't kill him, did you?"

"No, of course not," O'Day said. But then he smiled and said, "But he ain't gonna wake up for a while."

"How did Spenser die?"

"He was shot."

"Find out where he lived?"

O'Day nodded and said, "And he had a business, the hardware store."

"Okay," Kennedy said, looking at all of his men who were with him. "Soc and I will take the store. Wesley should be at the saloon. Find him and you all take the house. You'll have to break in, but do it *quietly*."

"What are we lookin' for?" O'Day asked.

Kennedy gave him a look and said, "If I knew that, then we wouldn't have to look for it."

After he gave Kennedy and Valdez directions, O'Day and the other men moved away and into the shadows.

"What *are* we lookin' for?" Valdez asked as they walked to the hardware store. "The man's dead."

"Maybe he left something behind," Kennedy

said, "something that will lead us to the boy."

"We don't even know if the boy was here."

"Adams is here," Kennedy said. "That's good enough for me."

Clint and Earthquake left the saloon, which was virtually a shambles. Men were still laughing, even though they were afraid of Earthquake. It was just too funny for them *not* to laugh. He, in turn, had gotten to his feet with a hurt look on his face, and Clint had ushered him out.

"That wasn't so funny," the big man complained outside. "I could have got hurt."

Clint, trying to suppress a grin *and* a laughing fit of his own, said, "You're right, Earthquake. They're just rude people."

"You said it," Earthquake said.

"Listen," Clint said, "while you were rolling around on the floor Kennedy's man left. He's probably going to warn them."

"About what?"

"About us," Clint said.

"What for? We don't even know what he's doin' right now."

"That's just it," Clint said. "I think I do. Come on."

THIRTY-FOUR

Earthquake hurried after Clint in the dark.

"How could you know where they are?" he wanted to know. "We were sitting in the saloon together and *I* don't know where they are."

"It's just logical, Earthquake," Clint said.

"Call me Quake."

"Well," Clint said, "*that's* helpful. Okay, Quake, there are only two places in this town that Lloyd Kennedy and his boys would be interested in."

"The whorehouse and the saloon?"

"No," Clint said. "That would be if they weren't working, but they are."

"So what are the two places?"

"Spenser's house," Clint said, "and his store."

"So which one do we go to?"

"I want you to go to Spenser's house," Clint

said. "Have a look around—and be careful."

"What am I looking for?" the big man asked.

"Nothing," Clint said, "but Kennedy's men might be there looking for something. If they are, I want to know about it."

"Oh, I get it," Earthquake said. "You want me to *sneak* over there. And if they're there, you don't want them to see me."

"Right."

"You can count on me," Earthquake said.

An image of Earthquake destroying the inside of the saloon flashed into Clint's mind, but at least there would be no chairs in his way at Spenser's house.

"Where are you going?" Earthquake asked.

"I'm going to the store," Clint said. "That's where Kennedy will be."

"How do you know that?"

"I don't," Clint said, "but Spenser was killed there. If I was Kennedy that's where I would go."

"Where do we meet?"

"Back at the hotel."

"When?"

"As soon as you're done."

"All right," Earthquake said, clapping his hands together enthusiastically. "Let's get to work."

The sound of his hands coming together sounded almost like thunder.

As Clint approached the late Victor Spenser's hardware store he thought he detected some light inside. It would be pitch black inside, so a candle, or a lamp, would be absolutely necessary for anyone searching.

He moved to the window and looked inside. There were two men there, and while they were trying to be careful to cover the glow of the lamp, Clint was able to see that they were Lloyd Kennedy and Soc Valdez. He was relieved. He'd been worried that Earthquake might run into these two. It was better that the big lawman would have to deal with Kennedy's men, and not the leader of the pack himself.

That was how Clint thought of Kennedy and his men, as a wolf leader and his pack.

Clint checked the front door, and it looked secure and not tampered with. He assumed that Kennedy and Valdez had used the back door. That meant they would come out the same way.

He found an alley that would take him to the back of the building, and waited there for them.

"This would be a lot easier if we knew what we were looking for," Soc Valdez grumbled.

Kennedy stood straight up and looked around. There was no point in tearing the place apart. Spenser had been killed unexpectedly. He wouldn't have had time to hide anything important. If there was going to be something that would lead them to the younger Spenser, it would have to be out in the open.

Only it wasn't.

"All right," Kennedy said, "forget it, Soc."

Valdez dropped the papers he was looking at and stood straight up.

"We givin' up?" he asked.

"Only here," Kennedy said. "Come on, let's get the others and get out of town. We'll camp up on that ridge you were watching from."

"And then what?" Valdez asked. "We gonna follow Adams again?"

"I'll have to think that over tonight," Kennedy said. "With the father dead he might be facing the same wall we are. If that's the case, then he can't help us anymore. We'll get to the kid before he does on our own."

Valdez shrugged and followed Kennedy to the rear door, the way they had come in. They'd had to damage the door, but since it was the *back* door, and the store would be closed for a while anyway, they'd figured it would be a long time before anyone noticed.

Kennedy opened the door and whispered to Valdez, "Douse the lamp."

Before Valdez could, however, someone said, "Why put it out? We could use the light."

Clint spoke mainly to announce his presence. He didn't want to surprise either man and have him go for his gun. That would have only led to a real mess.

As it was, Valdez *did* go for his gun, but Clint could see Kennedy react a lot more coolly. In fact, the man had obviously recognized his voice.

"Easy, Soc," Kennedy said, putting his hand on Valdez's gun hand. "It's our friend, Mr. Adams."

"Friend is stretching the truth a little, Kennedy," Clint said. "In fact, it's stretching it a lot."

"What are you doing here, Adams?" Kennedy asked.

"I figured you and your men would be out late tonight, doing a little looting."

"We ain't loo—"

"Mr. Adams knows what we're doing, Soc," Kennedy said. "He's just making a little joke at our expense."

"Find anything interesting, Kennedy?"

"I could say yes," Kennedy said, "but what's the point of lying. We didn't find a thing."

"I didn't think you would," Clint said. "I don't think the boy's father knew where he went when he left here. In fact, I think he might even have sent him away."

"Care to tell me why you think that?" Kennedy asked.

Clint hesitated, then said, "How about we talk over a drink?"

"Sure," Kennedy said, "why not. You know what? I'll even buy."

THIRTY-FIVE

The three men left the area of the hardware store and walked towards the saloon.

"You might want to send Valdez here to Spenser's house to get your other men."

Kennedy stared at Clint for a moment, then smiled and turned to Valdez.

"You heard Mr. Adams, Soc," he said. "Go and collect the men and I'll meet you in camp."

"But I should stay—"

"Go," Kennedy said. "Mr. Adams and I are just gonna talk, aren't we, Clint?"

"That's right, Soc," Clint said. "Just some talk."

"See?" Kennedy said. "I'll be just fine."

"Soc, you might want to watch out for the sheriff," Clint said. "Actually, he's so big you probably can't miss him, but he should be trying to pussyfoot around the house without alerting your men."

"I'll keep my eyes open," Valdez said.

"No surprises, Soc," Kennedy said, wagging his finger at the man. "Let's not get into any hasty gun battles with the law, all right?"

"Sure, Boss."

Valdez left to go to the house, and Clint and Kennedy continued on to the saloon.

As they entered Clint noticed that the mess Earthquake had made had been cleaned up and order restored. However, people still looked at him funny, and looked *behind* him to see if the big man was with him.

"Do I have egg on my face?" Kennedy asked.

"They're not looking at you," Clint said. "They're looking at me—that is, they're looking for my big friend, the sheriff."

"Oh, yeah?" Kennedy said. "Did he made an impression?"

Clint had to laugh as he said, "Oh, yeah, he made a *big* impression."

Clint started for the bar, but was intercepted by Mitzi, the red-haired saloon girl.

"That's okay, sweetie," she said. "Just sit at a table and I'll bring you your drinks."

"Beer?" Clint asked Kennedy.

"Fine."

"Two," Clint told Mitzi.

"Comin' up, sweetie," she said.

"I see our big friend isn't the only one who's made an impression," Kennedy said.

Clint ignored the comment and led the way to an open table.

"I guess you'll be heading out tomorrow morning," Kennedy said as they sat.

"I guess so."

"Going which way?"

"Your guess is as good as mine."

"You'll forgive me if I think my experience makes my guess *better* than yours?"

"You're forgiven," Clint said.

Mitzi arrived with the two beers, set them down, pressed her hip against Clint's shoulder, smiled, and flounced away.

"Women like you, don't they?" Kennedy asked.

Clint didn't answer. He wondered what kind of conversation would take place if he left Kennedy and Earthquake together.

"All right," Kennedy said. "I guess we're both in the same situation here."

"You had me followed from Broken Back figuring I'd lead you to the father," Clint said.

Kennedy shrugged and said, "It seemed the logical thing to do. Did you see my man?"

"No," Clint said, "but I know Valdez's talents. I figured if he was following me I wasn't going to see him anyway."

"So you led him here planning to do what?" Kennedy asked.

Clint shrugged. "He didn't have to know this was our destination," he said. "I was hoping to make it look like we were just stopping for supplies. When I found out that Spenser was dead, though, it didn't matter anymore."

"Yes," Kennedy said, "the fact that he's dead does make it harder on all of us, doesn't it?"

"Yeah, it does."

"How was he killed?"

Clint didn't hesitate, because he knew the question was going to come up, and he had already decided how to answer it.

"The bank robbers killed him."

Kennedy's hand froze as he was bringing his beer to his mouth. He hesitated, then lifted it the rest of the way, took a thoughtful sip, and set it down again.

"That's interesting," he said finally. "How did you find out about that? The local law?"

"The local law isn't interested in who killed him," Clint said. He went on to tell Kennedy about his talk with Sheriff Bennett, and how he subsequently located a witness to the incident.

"Sounds like you did all the sheriff's work for him," Kennedy said.

"Let him find his own witness."

Kennedy thought for a moment, then gestured with his hand when he said, "Okay, so let me see how you figure this. The kid tried to double-cross his partners and came here with the money. The father didn't like the idea of his kid being a thief and tossed him out. The gang showed up and killed the father."

"That's it."

"So the kid's running from you, me, *and* his own gang," Kennedy said.

"That's the way it looks."

"It *looks* like a mess," Kennedy said.

"It could be," Clint said.

"Yeah," Kennedy said, "if we all come together in the same place at the same time."

"There's a way we can avoid the mess, though," Clint said.

Kennedy looked at him and said, "You mean by working together?"

Clint nodded.

Kennedy made an apologetic face, sucking some air between his teeth, and said, "I don't think I can do that." The words came out haltingly, as if he was forcing them out against his will.

"Why not?" Clint asked. "I'm not looking for a piece of your . . . fee."

"Oh, very good, Clint," Kennedy said with a smile. "You almost called it a bounty, but caught yourself."

"Whatever it is," Clint said, "I don't want any part of it. I only want to keep that boy alive until his mother can find out what really happened."

"Well," Kennedy said, "*we* already know what happened. If he's running from the gang, it means he *was* in on the robbery. In fact, *he* has the money. There's not much doubt left that he's guilty."

"And he'll probably go to prison," Clint said, "if he lives that long, but before that happens I want to give his mother a chance to talk to him. She'll need to do that if she's going to come to terms with this thing."

Kennedy turned his beer mug around and around on the table.

"I'd really like to help you there, Clint, I really would," Kennedy said, "but I have to be concerned with the rights of my client. I can't worry about the kid, *or* his mother. You understand."

Clint frowned and said, "No, I don't, Kennedy. You come off as an intelligent man, not at all bloodthirsty."

"Like my rep, you mean?"

"That's right."

"And what about you?" Kennedy asked. "You don't seem like the killer your rep makes you out to be."

"I'm not."

"So should we sit here and try to explain it to each other?"

"No," Clint said, and abruptly stood up. "Thanks for the drink."

"Don't go away mad, Clint . . ." Kennedy was saying, but Clint kept walking until he was out the door and didn't hear the rest.

THIRTY-SIX

When Clint got back to his hotel Earthquake was sitting in the lobby. He looked a little disheveled, but none the worse for wear. In fact, he looked very pleased with himself.

As Clint entered Earthquake stood up from the sofa he was sitting on. Behind him the sofa sagged in the middle, having never had to put up with anything like the big man's bulk before. The look on the desk clerk's face said it all. Somebody was going to have to buy a new sofa.

"What happened to you?" Clint asked.

"I did just what you said," Earthquake said, already sounding like he was making excuses for something he had done. "I sneaked over to the Spenser house to take a look around."

"And?"

"They were in there, all right. I could see

lights, and they weren't being too quiet about it. I think they pretty much wrecked the inside of the house."

"Did you go inside?"

"No," Earthquake said, holding up his right hand. "I swear, Clint, I didn't go inside. They made *that* mess themselves."

Clint hesitated, then said, "*That* mess? What other mess was there?"

"Well," Earthquake said, "there's the window. I mean, that's the only *thing* that's *really* damaged."

"What window?"

"It wasn't my fault," he said. "When they came out and saw me they went for their guns."

"I didn't hear any shots."

"Oh, there weren't any," Earthquake said. "See, I reached out pushed the one closest to me—just a little. He went backwards into one of the others, and they *both* went through a window."

"You pushed him . . . just a little?"

"That's right."

"And he *and* one of the other men went through the window?"

"Right," Earthquake said, as if it all made perfect sense. "They were real careless."

"I'll bet," Clint said. "What happened then?"

"Well, the third one, he *got* his gun out. I was able to keep him from firing at me."

"How'd you do that?"

"I, uh, broke his arm."

"Broke it . . . how bad?"

"Well . . . I didn't mean it. See, I just *grabbed* his arm so he wouldn't shoot, and I heard two cracks, so I guess it snapped in two places."

"*Two* places."

"Right."

"What about the guy from the saloon," Clint asked. "Did he show up too?"

"Yeah," Earthquake said, "but I took care of him too."

Clint closed his eyes and asked, "What did you do to him?"

"I told him not to shoot, and he didn't," Earthquake said. "I *thought* he was being cooperative, but when he got close enough he tried to club me with his gun. See?"

Earthquake bent over so Clint could see the lump on his head.

"So he *did* club you," Clint said.

"Well, yeah, but he wasn't too strong, so it didn't hurt that much. Of course, I didn't want him to hit me *again,* so . . ."

"So . . . what?"

"I stopped him."

"How?" Clint said, almost afraid to ask.

"I grabbed the hand he was holding the gun in."

Clint waited a few moments, then said, "And?"

"Well . . . *something* broke, because he started to yell, and when I let him go the gun fell to the ground and he held his hand in his lap."

"And what were the two fellas who went through the window doing by this time?" Clint asked.

"They, uh, hadn't gotten up yet."

"Do you know how badly they were hurt?"

"Well, I *would* have found out, but by that time the Mexican one with the funny name came along."

"You didn't hurt him, did you?"

"No, he was *real* reasonable," Earthquake said. "He looked his men over and then told me I'd better go. He'd take care of everything."

Clint put his arm around the man's huge shoulders and said, "Quake, it sounds like you just about wiped out Kennedy's whole pack."

"Well . . . I didn't mean to," the big man said. "I was just, you know, protecting myself. I didn't *mean* to hurt any of 'em."

"No," Clint said, "I know you didn't."

Clint couldn't imagine the kind of damage Earthquake might have done if he *had* meant it.

"Come on, Earthquake," Clint said, "we might as well go upstairs."

"Did you talk to Kennedy?" Earthquake asked. "What did *you* find out?"

"I'll tell you all about it, Quake," Clint said, "upstairs."

About an hour later there was a knock on Clint's door. He had sent Earthquake back to his own room after relaying his conversation with Lloyd Kennedy. He'd told the big man to get some sleep, because they'd be heading out early the next morning.

"Where to?" Earthquake had asked.

"I'm not sure about that just yet."

Now when he opened the door he expected to see Earthquake standing there, or maybe even the red-haired saloon girl. What he *wasn't* expecting to see was Lloyd Kennedy.

"Kennedy," Clint said. "To what do I owe this pleasure?"

"Is that offer to join forces still open?" Kennedy asked.

"What happened to change your mind?"

Kennedy gave Clint an exasperated look and said, "It seems my men ran into an earthquake."

Clint stared at the man for a few moments. Kennedy was almost a comic figure right then, standing in the hall looking forlorn and lost. A wolf without his pack.

"Let's go and get a drink," Clint said.

THIRTY-SEVEN

"What's the damage?" Clint asked.

"Clyde and Harve are cut up," Kennedy said, "plus Clyde's got a stove-in rib."

Clint flinched, but didn't say anything. They were back in the saloon, different table but same red-haired saloon girl bringing them their drinks. Kennedy continued the inventory of injuries.

"Henny O'Day's got a broken arm, broke in two places," he said. "Wilson's got some broken fingers. Doc says he's lucky his hand wasn't crushed. He wanted to know what Wilson had gotten his hand stuck in to do that kind of damage."

Clint didn't know what to say.

"You know what they told me?"

"What?"

"They said the man wasn't even mad at them," Kennedy said, with disbelief in his tone. "They said he was almost matter-of-fact about it."

"He was just trying to protect himself, Kennedy," Clint said. "He said that when he surprised them they went for their guns."

"Yeah," Kennedy said, "and they said he moved faster than anyone that size should be able to move."

"Well . . . he's a surprising man," Clint said.

"I'd say so, yeah," Kennedy said.

"What about Valdez? What's he got to say?"

"He says he got there after the fact," Kennedy said. "The others were just lying around, moaning and groaning. He said your friend looked *lost,* as if he hadn't even been there when the carnage happened, like he'd just walked in on it. Could it be he didn't know what he'd done?"

"Maybe he didn't know while he was doing it," Clint said, "but he told me about it afterward. He seemed genuinely . . . surprised at what he'd done. I don't think the man has a malicious bone in his body."

"Jesus!" Kennedy said. "If he had he probably would have killed them all."

"I would have," Clint said. "If it had been me and they went for their guns, I would have had to protect myself the only way I knew how. That's what he did."

"Well," Kennedy said, "I've only got myself and Valdez now, and even not counting the kid there are still five other bank robbers. If that offer of yours to join forces is still good, I think I'll take you up on it."

"Well, well," Clint said, "a historic day."

"I'm not splitting the money with you, though," Kennedy said.

"I told you I didn't want the money," Clint said, "and I meant it."

"Okay."

"But there's something else."

Kennedy made a face and said, "A catch."

"Right."

"What is it?"

"The kid," Clint said. "I want him to have every chance to live."

Kennedy rubbed his jaw.

"You know, if I'm not willing to totally defend myself," Kennedy said, "that gives an edge to the other person."

"I'll tell you what," Clint said. "I'll make you another offer."

"What offer?"

"When we catch up to the kid," Clint said slowly, "if it comes down to you or him . . . I'll kill him myself."

Kennedy was taken by surprise. He sat back in his chair and stared at Clint for a long time.

"You're serious," he said finally. "You really mean it."

"Yes."

Kennedy leaned forward and put out his hand, and Clint took it.

"Done," Kennedy said.

THIRTY-EIGHT

Clint left Kennedy in front of the saloon. Kennedy was going to go and check on his men, and then get hotel rooms for them as well as for himself and Valdez. The men would have to stay in Dayville to recover from their injuries. He and Valdez would be ready to move out at first light.

Clint went back to the hotel and knocked on Earthquake's door. The big man answered the door almost immediately.

"Did I wake you?" Clint asked.

"No," Earthquake said. "If I was sleeping you would have had to kick the door to wake me. Is there something wrong?"

"I thought you might want a report on Kennedy's men," Clint said. He gave Earthquake the rundown of injuries he had caused, and the man looked more and more sheepish until Clint was done.

"Jeez," Earthquake said, "I didn't mean to do all that, Clint, I really didn't."

"I know you didn't, Quake," Clint said. "You should be happy to know that none of them are *seriously* hurt, but they won't be riding for a while."

"I guess that just leaves Kennedy and the Mexican, huh?" Earthquake said.

"And us."

"Us?"

"We're going to be combining our talents, Earthquake," Clint said. "Tomorrow morning you, me, Valdez, and Kennedy will be riding out together."

"Well . . . that *sounds* okay, except for one thing," the big man said.

"What?"

He looked sad and said, "I don't *have* any talents."

Clint put his hand on Earthquake's shoulder and said, "Don't underestimate yourself, my friend."

Clint told Earthquake to go to sleep and he'd wake him early the next morning.

"Don't forget," Earthquake said. "Kick the door."

"I'll remember."

He went back to his own room and started to

get undressed for bed. He was bare-chested and barefoot when there was a knock on his door again. Lloyd Kennedy again? Earthquake?

No, this time it *was* the red-haired saloon girl.

THIRTY-NINE

"Mitzi," he said.

"You remembered," she said.

"Sure, I remembered."

She raked her eyes over his chest and then said, "Aren't you gonna ask me in?"

He stuck his head out the door and looked up and down the hall.

"What about your reputation?" he asked.

She smiled and said, "What reputation?"

Her skin was pale all over. She had small breasts, but they were firm, and she had big pink nipples that reacted to the slightest touch. They tightened when he just breathed on them, and when he took them in his mouth she went wild underneath him.

Soon after she entered the room she began to

undress him. Of course, he'd had a head start, so all she had to do was remove his pants and underwear. When she finished, she went on her knees in front of him, and her mouth swooped down on him and captured him inside.

He took hold of her head while she rode him with her mouth, sucking him wetly, and when he knew he was in danger of exploding he grabbed her and pulled her to her feet. At that point he peeled off her clothes, lifted her up—she was *light*—and carried her to the bed.

She was slim all over, but her body was firm, well toned. She managed slimness without being skinny, something not a lot of women were able to do. It occurred to him that she was very young, but he decided not to think about that until later.

He just concentrated on the task at hand . . .

In the middle of the night Clint woke with a start. After he and Mitzi had made love for the second time she had drifted off to sleep on his chest. He had taken the time to think over Will Spenser's situation. With his father turning him away, where would he go next?

He'd fallen asleep with that question on his mind . . . and awakened with the answer.

Mitzi had slid off his chest, but her head was still on his shoulder, and she had one pale, slender, well-toned leg slung over him. He slid out from beneath her without waking her, dressed, and went downstairs.

The desk clerk was dozing, and he woke him by prodding him none too gently.

"Huh? Wha—"

"I need a room number."

"You got a room a'ready," the man muttered.

"Not *my* room," Clint said, impatiently. "Lloyd Kennedy. What room is he in?"

"Who?"

"Ah . . ." Clint pushed the man away and grabbed the register book. He looked up Kennedy's name, noted the room number, and went back upstairs. He found the man's room and pounded on the door.

"What the fuck," Kennedy said, swinging the door open. "Adams? What the hell is wr—"

"I've got it!" Clint said.

"Got what?"

"I know where the kid went."

Kennedy blinked, then wiped his eyes with both palms. He dropped his hands and looked at Clint again.

"Okay, where?"

"He came here to see his father," Clint said, "right? To get his help?"

"Yeah . . . right, so?"

"And the old man wouldn't help him."

"Yeah, yeah," Kennedy said impatiently.

"So who's the only person left now who could help him?" Clint asked.

"Shit," Kennedy said, scratching his head, "I don't know—"

"Come on, Kennedy," Clint said excitedly.

"Who's the only person in his life who *would* help him, no matter *what* he did?"

Kennedy stared at Clint, and then stopped scratching his head. "His mother?"

"Right."

"Shit," Kennedy said. "The little shit's gone back to Broken Back."

"There's no place else for him to go," Clint said. "It makes sense."

"It makes a lot of sense," Kennedy said. "Hell, I wish I'd've thought of it."

"It doesn't matter who thought of it," Clint said. "We'll head back come morning."

"Early," Kennedy said.

"Real early," Clint said.

"Can I go back to sleep now?"

"We can both go back to sleep now."

FORTY

Clint woke with first light streaming through the window. Sleeping with Mitzi had been so warm and comfortable that he'd overslept. Jesus Christ, he thought, wiping his face, he was getting old. There was no doubt about it.

"Whatsamatta?" Mitzi asked as he leaped out of bed.

"I'm late," he said, "I've got to go."

"A'ready?"

"Sorry," he said. He dressed quickly, then bent over and kissed the back of her neck, where her red hair tapered down. He wondered why she wore it so short, but didn't have time to ask.

"Come back . . ." she said, but he was out the door and rushing down the hall. He hated to run out on her so fast, but he had a bad feeling . . .

He pounded on Earthquake's door, and then

finally started kicking it. The big man had been right. That was what it took to wake him.

"Get dressed," Clint said when the man came to the door.

"What time is it?"

"Late," Clint said. "Get dressed."

Clint hurried down the hall to Lloyd Kennedy's door and banged on it. When there was no answer he braced himself against the opposite wall and kicked out. The door shattered around the doorknob and swung open.

The room was empty.

"That sonofabitch!"

About two hours outside of Dayville Soc Valdez asked Kennedy, "Ain't you worried about what he's gonna do?"

"No."

"But . . . you agreed to work together," Valdez said. "That was the reason he shared his information, his opinion with you."

Kennedy looked over at Valdez and said, "Soc, have you ever known me to *share* anything with anyone if I didn't want to?"

"No."

"Well, I'm not about to share this," Kennedy said. "Sure, Adams figured out where the kid was going, but now that we've got that information, it'd be stupid not to act on it."

"He'll catch up, though."

"Yeah," Kennedy said, grinning, "he will, won't he? Won't that be interesting?"

• • •

It didn't take long for Clint to determine that the bad feeling he'd woke up with was on the money. Kennedy's other men were still in their rooms in the hotel, but Kennedy himself and Soc Valdez were gone.

"You can't blame yourself," Earthquake said while they saddled their horses.

Clint had been cursing himself out loud the whole time he was saddling Duke. "No? Who can I blame?"

"He agreed to work together—"

"He lied," Clint said, "and I was stupid enough to believe him. I let the smooth, slimy bastard take me, Earthquake. That hasn't happened to me in a long time . . . a *very* long time."

The sonofabitch had taken *his* information and had run out on him.

Yeah, he was getting old, all right.

FORTY-ONE

Jeannie Spenser was shocked when her son, Will, showed up on her doorstep. It had been about ten days since the bank robbery, and she was starting to think that she would never see her son again.

"Oh, my God!" she said when she saw him at the door.

She opened the door and reached out to embrace him. He stood stiffly within the circle of her arms, his own arms hanging down at his sides. Hanging from his right hand was a big sack.

"Come inside," she said suddenly, pulling him into the house. She was afraid someone would see him. "Are you all right?"

"I'm fine."

"Where have you been?" she asked. "Are you hungry? What's that you're holding?"

"Ma," Will said, "Jesus, Ma, will you stop?"

"Will?" He had never talked to her like that before. "What is it?" She looked at the curious sack again and said, "What is it? What's in the sack?"

"What do you think?" he asked.

He untied the leather thong around the neck of the sack, upended it, and dumped the contents out onto the floor, shaking it so that every last dollar bill would flutter out.

"Oh, my God!" Jean Spenser said.

FORTY-TWO

Sam Cade couldn't believe it.

"We're back where the whole thing started," he said to the others.

Avery and Carl Dalman nodded. Carl's arm was still in a sling from the wound he'd received the day of the robbery.

"This is where the money is," Carl said, "again, so this is where we are."

Jimmy Payne and Joe Daniels both nodded.

"This time," Cade said, "there won't be any mistakes. I want the money, and I want that kid dead. *I* want to be the one who kills him. Understand?"

"Sure, Sam," Daniels said.

"You get the kid," Jimmy Payne said.

The Dalman boys nodded their agreement.

"Okay," Cade said. "Let's go get our money."

• • •

Jeannie Spenser couldn't believe it. Will had been home two days, and she still couldn't believe that he had actually been in on the robbery. And what was *worse* was that he actually seemed *proud* of it—and of the fact that he had then turned around and stolen the money from his five partners.

"Those men are not just going to let you get away with it, Will," she said.

They were sitting in the kitchen, having just finished breakfast. Luckily there were no boarders in the house. There hadn't been any for a week.

"They don't know where I am, Ma," Will said, having another cup of coffee. "They'll never come back here lookin' for me. They're too stupid for that."

Jean Spenser didn't know what to say. Suddenly, her little boy had grown up, and he was a chief. Was it her fault? Was it because he hadn't had a father around when he was growing up?

"Did you see him, Will?" she asked.

He didn't answer right away, but when he did he looked right at her.

"My father? Oh, yeah, I saw him."

"How does he . . . look?"

"He looks fine, Ma," Will said, "but he sure as hell didn't want me around. He made that *real* clear."

"Did you tell him what you'd done?"

"Sure, I told him," Will said. "I thought he'd be . . . impressed."

"Did you?" she asked incredulously. "Did you really?"

"Ma, you don't understand," Will said. "What I did took guts, and brains. You don't just plan a robbery and then steal the money from your partners. That all takes advance planning."

"You planned to do that from the very beginning?" she asked.

"That's right," he said, "and look how it paid off. There's a lot of money there, Ma."

"I don't want to know how much," she said, holding her hand up. "All I know is that it's going back to the bank today."

"What?"

"That's right," she said. "Maybe if you give it back, Mr. Kennedy and Mr. Adams will stop looking for you."

"Kennedy?" Will said. "Adams? Who are they?"

Jean Spenser told her son about the dangerous men who were hunting for him.

"Mr. Adams wants to bring you in alive, but he's afraid that Mr. Kennedy doesn't want the same thing," she finished. "And now you probably have those . . . *partners* of yours looking for you as well. No, the best thing to do is return the money, and then maybe we'll even be able to keep you out of jail."

"Ma," Will said, "I ain't givin' the money back."

"But . . . you must!"

"Ma," Will said, "a man was *killed* during the robbery. I'm not wanted only for bank robbery,

I'm wanted for *murder*!"

"But you didn't kill him . . . did you?"

"No," Will said, "I didn't pull the trigger. That was one of the others. But that doesn't matter. We're *all* wanted for murder."

"Then . . . then why did you come back?" she asked.

"I need a place to hide," he said. "What could be a better place than home? No one will *ever* think of looking here. Pretty smart, huh?"

Before she could answer there was the sound of breaking glass from the front of the house as something came flying through the window.

"What the hell," he said. He got up, grabbed his gun, and ran toward the front window. Jean Spenser was close behind him.

"What is it?" she asked.

"I don't know," he said, looking at the rock on the floor amid the broken glass, and then looking out the window. And then he saw who was outside waiting for him. "Shit."

"Come on out, Will!" Sam Cade called out. "Come out and your mother won't get hurt."

"Who is that, Will?"

"Sam Cade," Will said, "and the others."

"Others?"

He turned and said, "The other bank robbers, Ma. They're all out there, and they want *me*!"

FORTY-THREE

"What the hell," Lloyd Kennedy said, reining his horse in hard.

Soc Valdez stared ahead of them and said, "How the hell did they get ahead of us?"

Both men sat their horses quietly as Clint Adams and Earthquake Nolan rode up on them. When they got close enough Kennedy asked the question for Valdez.

"You were only a couple of hours ahead of us, Kennedy," Clint said, "and Sheriff Nolan here knew a nice little shortcut."

"So what now? Now that you're here, I mean," Kennedy said.

"You're a bastard, Kennedy," Clint said, but he said it without anger. He had come to terms with his anger already, and was determined not to let it affect his actions. "But I'm going to make you keep your word. We're going to ride into Broken Back together and bring that boy in."

Kennedy wiped his mouth with his thumb and forefinger, thinking.

"All right, Clint."

"Don't call me by my first name, Kennedy," Clint snapped at him.

"All right, *Mr. Adams,*" Kennedy said, "we'll ride into town together. Beyond that, though, I'm not making any promises."

"It wouldn't matter if you did," Clint said. "You don't *keep* your promises, remember?"

"Time to come out, Will," Sam Cade called out to Will Spenser.

Next to him Jimmy Payne asked, "What if he ain't in there?"

"He's in there, all right," Cade said. "I can feel him, and I can smell the money. He's in there."

"Well," Payne said, "if he's in there, how come he ain't sayin' nothin'?"

"He'll say something," Cade said. "Let's put some lead into the walls."

Cade opened fire, and the others followed his example. Before long lead was chewing chunks out of the front of the house.

Inside, Will Spenser hit the floor as the bullets starting poking glass out of all the windows. He gave no thought at all to his mother, and if she hadn't had the presence of mind to hit the floor, she would have surely been killed.

When the shooting stopped, Will lifted his head and listened. Glass fell from his hair and his shoulders as he pushed himself to a kneeling position.

"Will," Jean Spenser said, brushing glass off herself, "what do we do?"

"I don't know," Will said, sounding like a little boy. "I don't know *what* to do, Ma."

She stared at her son with new eyes and said harshly, "What happened, Will? I thought you had it all figured out in advance."

"Not this," he said, shaking his head and looking frightened, "not this . . ."

As Clint, Earthquake, Kennedy, and Valdez were approaching the town of Broken Back they heard the volley of shots.

"Well," Kennedy said, looking at Clint, "it sounds like everybody is here."

FORTY-FOUR

The shots had stopped by the time Clint and the others came riding within sight of town.

"Now, where did the shots come from?" Soc Valdez asked aloud.

"Where else?" Clint asked.

"The Spenser house," Kennedy said.

"Right."

They urged their horses into a run and directed them through town, right down the main street to the south end, where the Spenser boardinghouse was located.

"There!" Clint said, pointing across from the house to where five men had taken cover.

Suddenly the five men opened fire on the house again.

"Looks like they could use some help," Kennedy said, drawing his gun.

"Let's do this right—" Clint started to say, but Kennedy and Valdez started riding, firing at the five men, before he could finish.

"Shit," Clint said, and took off after them, with Earthquake right behind him.

Sam Cade heard the shots and looked to his right. Four men were riding down on them.

"Shit," Jimmy Payne said, also seeing.

"What do we do?" Joe Daniels.

There had been no return fire from the house at all, so Sam Cade said, "Come on."

"Where?" Avery Dalman asked.

"The house," Cade said. "Now!"

When Clint saw the five men break for the house, his worst fears were realized. If Kennedy had waited long enough they could have caught the robbers in a cross fire and kept them from running for the house. Now he watched as the men charged the house, and either broke down the front door or dove through the glassless windows.

He caught up to Kennedy, who had reined in, and said, "This is great. Now they're inside, probably with the kid and his mother. And who knows how many boarders are in there."

"We'll get them out," Kennedy said, ejecting spent shells from his gun and replacing them. "At least we know where they all are now."

"Listen, Kennedy," Clint said, "we've got to do this together. We don't have enough men to go against each other on this."

Kennedy looked at Clint, who was also replacing shells in his gun, and said, "Just do what I say, Adams, and this will work out."

"And they'll all end up dead, right?" Clint asked.

Kennedy shrugged and said, "That's their choice, isn't it?"

"No," Clint said, "I'm making it *my* choice."

With that he swung his gun and caught Kennedy on the head with the barrel. The man fell off his horse and hit the ground with a thud.

"Hey!" Valdez said, but before he could do anything Earthquake knocked him from his saddle by swinging one massive arm.

"Good work, Earthquake," Clint said.

"What do we do now?" the man asked.

"We're back in your town again, Sheriff," Clint said. "Get your deputies and toss these two in a cell. After that, we'll figure out what to do about the robbers. They're inside now, and at the very least they have Mrs. Spenser as a hostage."

"Unless she got out before they got here."

"Yeah," Clint said, "that would make it easier, wouldn't it?"

But even as he said it he knew they would have no such luck.

Inside the house Cade and his men disarmed Will Spenser, and then forced him and his mother to sit on the sofa.

"Get out of my house," Jeannie Spenser shouted.

"If she talks again," Cade told Jimmy Payne, "kill her."

"Sure," Payne said, swallowing hard. He'd never killed a woman before, and he didn't even know if Cade was serious about it.

"Here's the money," Avery Dalman said, finding the sack.

"Good," Cade said. "We've got the money, and we've got our young friend."

"That's great," Carl Dalman said, "but we also got trouble. How are we gonna get out of here?"

Cade looked around and said, "Hey, we got everything we want right here, Carl. They can't come in here because we got Momma here. She's gonna be our ticket out of here."

"And how do we punch that ticket?" Avery Dalman asked.

"Simple," Sam Cade said. "We just got to talk to the right person."

FORTY-FIVE

Earthquake dismounted, grabbed a foot in each hand, and dragged the two unconscious men off to jail.

"I'll be back," he called out.

"I'll be here," Clint promised.

He dismounted and walked over to where the robbers had previously taken cover behind some troughs.

"Hello, the house!"

"We're here," the reply came. "Who am I talking to?"

"My name's Clint Adams."

There was a long silence. With the amount of people who were in that house, it didn't surprise Clint that *somebody* recognized his name.

"What the hell are you doin' here?" the same voice finally asked.

"I'm just trying to help."

"Oh yeah?" the voice asked. "Who are you tryin' to help, Adams?"

"Everybody!"

"Can't be done," the voice said. "You're gonna have to settle for helpin' *us*. Are you speakin' for the law?"

"No," Clint said. "The sheriff will be here any minute . . . with his men."

"That's no good," the voice said. "I want to talk to the sheriff, but I don't want to see any of his men."

"Look, I can't—"

"If I see any other men besides you and him, I'll shoot the kid," the voice said.

"I thought he was one of you."

"He's a hostage," the voice said, "and so's his momma—only I'm savin' her for later. You understand?"

"I understand," Clint said. "Can I know who I'm talking to?"

There was a moment's hesitation, and then the voice said, "This here's Sam Cade."

Clint hadn't recognized Cade during the robbery, but he knew the name. The man was usually smart enough to use different men for different robberies. It made the gang harder to identify.

"You hear of me?" Cade asked. Obviously he was concerned with that, with being recognized. He probably figured he had the Gunsmith at his mercy, and he wanted everyone to know it was him.

Clint decided to play his game.

"I know who you are, Cade."

"That's good," Cade said, "that's *real* good, Adams. So now we both know who we're dealin' with. Who's that?"

Clint turned his head and saw Earthquake approaching with his two deputies.

"Get rid of them," Clint told Earthquake when the three men had reached him.

"What?"

"You and I are going to have to handle this," Clint said. "If he sees anyone else, he's going to start shooting in there."

"Is Mrs. Spenser in there?" Earthquake asked.

"Yes."

"Shit," Earthquake said. He looked at his two men and said, "Okay, get lost."

"Where?" Randy Russell asked.

"Just go to the end of the street where they can't see you," Clint said. "Be ready to move, though, when the sheriff says."

"Okay," Russell said. He looked at Pardee Hall and said, "Let's go."

As they moved away from the action Earthquake crouched down next to Clint.

"What's going on?"

"We've identified each other," Clint said. "They know who I am, and I know that the leader is Sam Cade."

Earthquake stared at Clint and asked, "Do we know who he is?"

"Yes," Clint said, and explained to the sheriff who Cade was.

"So what do we do now?"

"You'll have to negotiate with him."

"Negotiate? How?"

"We've got to get the woman out of there, Earthquake," Clint said. "We can't do anything while she's in danger of being hurt or killed."

"What if we just let them go?" the big man asked.

"I don't think that would work," Clint said. "They'd probably take her with them."

"So how do we get her away from them then?" Earthquake asked.

"I think there's only one way," Clint said.

"How's that?"

He looked at the big man and said, "Trade me for her."

FORTY-SIX

Cade wouldn't go for the trade. Instead, when Earthquake made the offer, Cade gave him his demands.

"I want our horses, and I want a clear path out of town," Cade said.

Clint and Earthquake exchanged glances.

"Should we let them go?" the big man asked.

"No," Clint said without hesitation. "They'll kill the hostages anyway."

"Why should we worry?" Earthquake asked.

"I'm not worried about the kid," Clint said, "but I *am* worried about the mother."

"So what do we do?"

"Tell them they'll get what they want, but it will take some time."

"What are you gonna do?"

"I'm going to work my way around to the back

and try to get into the house that way," Clint said. "If you hear shooting from inside, come running. Understand?"

"I understand."

"Give me as much time as you can before you start talking to them," Clint said, and hurried away.

Earthquake turned to face the house. He was as nervous as a groom at the end of a shotgun, but he knew what he had to do. If he *didn't* do his job, Clint Adams might pay the price for it, and he didn't want that.

He waited . . .

Clint took the long way around, circling several buildings and not just the house. He didn't want there to be any chance that he'd be spotted. He was almost to the back of the house when he heard the voices.

" . . . are you waitin' for?" he heard from Sam Cade. Then came Earthquake's reply. In his big, booming voice he explained that Cade's demands would be met, but that it would take a while.

" . . . better not take *too* long, you hear? We got hostages!"

Clint moved to the back of the house and flattened his back against it. If Cade had put a lookout here in the back he'd have little chance of succeeding at this, but Cade's talent seemed to be for robbing people, not holding them as hostages.

He looked in the kitchen window and saw that the room was empty. He went to the back door, but it was locked. It was flimsy, though, and by pressing his hip to it and pushing he managed to slip the lock. By holding it with his hand, he managed to keep the noise down as the door opened. He stopped and listened to see if he had been detected, and then entered.

He found himself in the darkened kitchen, and he could hear voices from the front room. He decided to play this fast, because thinking about it too long could be disastrous. He only had to hope that no one—like Jeannie Spenser herself—would see him and give him away.

Out front Earthquake was nervously waiting for something to happen. He had told Sam Cade that he would get him what he wanted but that he'd have to wait. Cade's reply was that he wouldn't wait too long.

Well, Earthquake, nervously squeezing the butt of his gun, was also hoping it wouldn't be too long.

"Sheriff!" Clint heard as he moved down the hallway to the front of the house. "What's takin' so long out there?" It was Cade. "I'll put a bullet in this woman's brain, don't think I won't."

Just as Clint came into the parlor he saw Sam Cade grab Jean Spenser by the hair, pull her up off the floor, and drag her to the window.

Damn! He had to act fast!

"Don't do it, Cade!"

Cade turned, looking around in surprise, and

when he saw Clint Adams he started to bring his gun to bear on him. He was partially shielded by the woman, but Clint knew he couldn't let that stop him.

He fired, and his bullet drilled Sam Cade in the forehead. The man's eyes went blank and his hands opened. His gun fell to the floor, and so did Jean Spenser.

Clint turned as the other men brought their guns around. He fired at one, hitting him in the chest, and then suddenly the front window exploded as Earthquake came crashing through it.

Clint fired again and another man fell.

Earthquake's arm lashed out and a man's nose exploded, gushing red all over the room, and *he* fell.

There was a fifth man, and he was trying to run for the door.

"Earthquake!" Clint shouted.

He had never seen a man that big move that fast. Before the last man could reach the door Earthquake was on him. He grabbed the man by the scruff of the neck, lifted him off his feet, and carried him back into the room.

Clint moved to Jean Spenser and helped her to her feet.

"Are you all right, Mrs. Spenser?"

"Yes," she said, looking around, "yes, I think I am. Wha-what happened?"

"Well," Clint said, "the sheriff made a bit of a mess, but he got the job done."

He took his hands from her shoulders, and she

took a few steps and looked down at her son. Will Spenser was still crouched down on the floor with his hands over his head. She reached down to touch him, but stopped short and then pulled her hand away.

"Will—what will happen to him?" she asked Clint.

"He was part of the robbery, Mrs. Spenser," Clint said. "He'll have to pay for that."

"Yes," she said, "yes, I suppose he will—I suppose he should . . . shouldn't he?"

"Yes, ma'am," Clint said. "He made a mistake and he *should* pay for it. Maybe he'll be a better man for it when he comes out of jail."

Clint didn't tell Jean Spenser that her son might *never* come out of jail since a man had been killed during the robbery. Why make her think about that now too? After all, she was about to lose her son—or maybe she'd already lost him.

"You know what?" Earthquake asked from behind Clint.

"What?" Clint asked.

"I think I've had enough of this job."

Clint looked at the big man and said, "I can't say I blame you, big fella. I can't say that I blame you."